They Are

Here Now

Short Tales

J.S. Lender (signature)

J.S. Lender

For Max, Emma, and Kaia

Contents

Down Below

FOLLOW ME, I want to show you something. I keep all the best ones down below.

Watch your step, and please excuse the mess. I was not expecting company today. It's quite cold and windy out there, isn't it? Oh yes, I do read quite a few magazines, but I haven't subscribed to anything for years. I ordered Rolling Stone once, but when I tried to cancel my subscription they kept sending me stuff in the mail like a creepy stalker.

You're sneezing already, are you allergic to cats? Come on down this way, let me turn on some lights so you can see where you're going. My cats are friendly, except for Ebeneezer over there. He swipes his claws without using much discretion. One time he caught me on the ankle while I was walking down the stairs, and I had cat scratch fever for three months. Cat scratch fever is a real thing, did you know that?

Do you have any pets? Well, that makes sense. You don't look like much of an animal person. I'll try not to hold that against you. Right down this way, if you don't mind.

When I first bought this house, the basement had been completely ruined by a busted pipe that flooded the entire downstairs. But I told my wife Betsy—she rests with the Good

Lord now, you understand—that I would get this basement fixed up real nice. She told me I could do whatever I wanted with the basement, as long as I watched all my Sunday football in there and kept all my manly stuff out of her sight. Betsy was a good woman, so I did as I was told.

The steps are a bit narrow and steep, so please be careful walking down. I don't need to get sued by some ambulance chasing son of a bitch lawyer! Oh goodness, please excuse my foul language. Betsy always made sure that I talked like a good boy, but with her gone, I slip up from time to time.

It's kind of cold and dark down here, I know. I am a sort of collector, you see. There's nothing I love more than God's furry little creatures. Most people think taxidermy is yucky, but I think it preserves the beauty of animals forever.

Over here is my bird collection. We have an old birdbath in the backyard. I always enjoyed drinking my morning coffee and watching the little critters from our kitchen window as they dipped their beaks in the water and ate from the birdfeeder.

After Betsy died, I mixed some rat poison in the birdfeeder. Oh, those little birds didn't really suffer, they would just fall over, stick up their tiny feet, and conk out.

I gathered myself a pretty nice collection of stuffed birds down here. See those up there? But they seemed so sad and lonely all by themselves.

So I dusted off the old .22 caliber rifle one day, and sure enough, it still looked to be in fine condition. With a few sandwiches packed and a jug of apple cider, I took myself on a little stroll into the woods.

You'd think that squirrels are quick, but not really. They just sit there like dumb rats, waiting to be shot. I got myself some nice fat ones, and mounted them up there on the wall. Look, see? I like the way their eyes follow you around the room.

But the squirrels seemed a bit lonely too, so I brought them down some friends. Come on over here, around the corner. This first fella was a Jehovah's Witness. Seemed like a nice enough guy at first, but they're all a bit shifty if you ask me. A Jehovah's Witness telling me I need to find Jesus, some nerve! I was a deacon in our church for 22 years!

He was mounted on the wall real nice too, see him up there at the top? The fella next to him was selling solar roof panels, of all things. I told him I didn't want no damn hippie plates on top of my house, but he tried to give me the hard sell! I haven't seen any salesman around here for a while. The economy ain't so good these days, I guess.

Where do you think you're going? I locked the door and there's no getting out of here without the key. Oh, come on now. You're starting to blubber just like the rest of them. What happened to all of the real men of the world, you know, the Clint Eastwood type? You should be flattered that I'm going to place you down here with the good looking ones. You should see all the ugly mugs I've got hanging in the upstairs attic. I keep all the best ones down below.

Why don't you come over here and sit a little bit closer, and tell me again about those magazines you're selling. If you show me something real good, maybe I'll let you go so I can get my magazines every month in the mail.

You got Good Housekeeping? They've got the best fondue recipes, if you ask me.

Two Rebel Girls

I MET THEM at a flea market on a hot, breezy August morning. A blonde and a brunette. Sisters. It was difficult not to stare, but I did my best. They strolled up next to me as I was flipping through a stack of old concert posters.

"I love Blues Traveler," said the blonde, eyeing the cardboard poster beneath my index finger.

"I guess they're okay, but I think John Popper just plays a bunch of notes on his harmonica really fast, if you ask me," said the brunette.

"Good thing no one's asking you," snapped the blonde.

"I like Blues Traveler too. John Popper doesn't just play a bunch of notes quickly, he's actually an accomplished harmonica player," I said, staring at both of them.

"If you're going to stare at us you might as well tell us your name. I'm Thelma, and this is Louise. Yes, just like the movie with Michael Madsen. Our mom had the hots for him, and she really liked how that movie ended. You know, two rebel girls doing things their own way."

"I'm Justin. I'm sorry for staring, I just haven't seen this before. Have you always been connected together?"

I felt my face get red with embarrassment from my idiotic

question, fearing that they had already pegged me as a dullard.

"LOL. Yes, we have always been conjoined twins, dummy. Two legs, two arms, and two heads should have been enough clues for you. Did you actually just ask us that?" said Thelma, laughing hysterically.

Thelma had been blessed with a warm, inviting smile and rows of perfectly straight white teeth. I admired that she had enough confidence to call me a dummy.

"I guess that helmet tucked under your arm means that you rode your motorcycle here? See how good we are at analyzing clues?" said Louise, with a smirk.

"Yea, I ride an old Triumph. Have you two ever been on a motorcycle?"

"What do you think?" asked Thelma.

"Why don't you guys let me take you out tonight. Give me your address and I'll pick you up at 7 o'clock."

"Ooooo, look at Mr. Confident," said Louise.

"What should we do with him," asked Thelma.

"I haven't decided yet," said Louise.

"All right dummy, here's our address. Bring two extra helmets."

"No problem, but there's one thing. You have to stop calling me dummy."

"You got it, Justin," said Louise, with a wink.

* * *

Thelma and Louise lived in a nice little townhouse in

Newport Coast. They greeted me at the door.

"Well, look who showed up. It's Easy Rider. Come on in, we're making White Russians."

"Do me a favor and go easy on the vodka. I don't want us to take a spill on the Triumph."

I wandered through their entryway, looking at framed photos hanging on the walls. Thelma and Louise had been up to all sorts of shenanigans. Parasailing. An African safari. Getting a kiss on the cheek from a seal at Sea World. The one constant in each of the photos were the smiles beaming from their happy faces.

I walked into the kitchen, sat on a barstool, and watched Thelma and Louise gracefully do their thing. Thelma tossed a few ice cubes and Louise caught them in a glass. Thelma's left arm poured vodka into the glass, while Louise's right arm poured Kahlúa in perfect tandem. Thelma finally topped it off with a generous portion of Half and Half.

"Here you go, Easy Rider," they said simultaneously, presenting the drink to me like a humanitarian award.

The White Russian was delicious, and I finished it in three gulps.

* * *

We rode onto Pacific Coast Highway, heading south. We must've been quite a sight—a row of three white helmets in triangle formation floating down the coastline. The sun was setting over Catalina Island and the ocean was a gleaming orange flame as we flew past Reef Point. A new swell was delivering endless rows of smooth, rolling waves toward El Morro cliff. The wind made everything go silent and the horizon looked as if it were reaching out for us. The palm trees passed us slowly at first, then in a blurry haze.

Thelma's left arm squeezed my stomach, as Louise's right arm squeezed a bit higher, at my ribs. Louise thrust her right thumb up. *Faster!* I pulled back on the throttle, and the roaring engine shot us through the California paradise of Laguna Beach.

I knew that upon our arrival at the bar there would be plenty of stares and whispers and pointing by strangers. Phones would be held in our direction and flashes would go off. Most likely, none of that would faze Thelma and Louise. It would all be new to me, though. But I found myself not caring, because I enjoyed being with both of them.

Enjoying Breakfast With the Devil

A FUNNY THING ABOUT THE DEVIL is that he enjoys a hot breakfast at a greasy diner just like everyone else. Lots of salt and pepper on his hash browns, an obnoxious pool of Tabasco sauce seeping through the center of his eggs, and a hefty pour of cream and sugar into a large mug of black coffee.

I decided to just call him "Devil," instead of pretending that he was someone else. The Devil and I met through my friend Lance. Lance owns a ferret and works as a bicycle mechanic. When I first met the Devil at a party at Lance's house, I noticed that his feet were small. His clothes were kind of shabby, but at the same time it looked as though his outfit had been carefully put together. His hair was dark and messy, with a bald spot on the crown of his head. The Devil was somewhat unkempt, with a few days of beard stubble. But his teeth were sparkly white. I sensed that it required considerable effort for the Devil to look like a slob.

The Devil and I hit it off right away, talking about politics, girls, cars, football, and beer. The only true disagreement between the Devil and myself during our first encounter concerned which female news anchor had the most epic breasts. After much back and forth, the Devil conceded that the blonde weather girl at 11 PM deserved to be the epic breast champion of network news. That's one of the things I admired about the Devil from the outset—he could admit when someone else was right.

It was getting late at Lance's party, and it was time to go home, so I shook hands with the Devil and gave him my business card.

* * *

The Devil called me two weeks later and invited me to breakfast at this diner called "The Magnificent Llama," on Pacific Coast Highway in Laguna Beach. I spotted him right away even though he was wearing a meticulously accessorized outfit with a scarf, a black button-down collared shirt, and tiny black lizard skin cowboy boots to protect his puny feet. His hair had been washed and he had shaved, which made him look younger but at the same time accentuated deep black wrinkles maneuvering about his face. We shook hands then sat at a booth with a celestial view of the Pacific Ocean.

The Magnificent Llama is a 50s diner with red vinyl booths. The walls are adorned with framed posters of Coca-Cola advertisements from the 1940s and 1950s. The old-fashioned ads show attractive women with perfect hair and makeup lounging poolside in conservative swimsuits. The women are casually sipping Coca-Cola through straws from a bottle, without a care in the world. The United States had just completed its mission of wiping the floor with the Nazis in World War II, and the only thing left to decide was which model Studebaker to purchase.

A young waitress with long black hair approached our table. The Devil complimented the waitress on her beautiful smile and dimples. She blushed. The Devil ordered breakfast for the two of us, then shooed the waitress away with the back of his hand.

We started chatting, but the Devil sensed something was wrong with me. He stopped talking and stared at me with a deep and strong gaze, calmly placing both of his hands onto the table, palms up.

"Place your hands on top of mine," he said.

The Devil's hands were smooth like calfskin. They were comfortably warm, too. I looked into his eyes as I grasped his hands, and a gentle calmness smothered me.

* * *

Within seconds, we were out of the diner. There were tall palm trees swaying back and forth, performing a choreographed dance. The wind blew strong and fast, but not a single hair on the Devil's head moved. The Devil stood stone still and gazed at me. A spotlight moon held the two of us tightly together in an eternal pact. It was the middle of the night and millions of stars were shining, but the sun was also burning brightly right there in the middle of the dead black sky. It was too dark to see anything, even with the bright sun and the spotlight moon, but I noticed green shadows scurrying back and forth along the beach.

The Devil handed me a comically large metal cup, and I drank something both sweet and bitter. I held hands with the Devil and we walked along the beach together, with the moon and sun shining on just the two of us in the dead of night like two spotlights on a stage.

* * *

As we were leaving the diner, the Devil gave me a great big warm hug.

"Let's meet Saturday night at The Beatnik Bar in Newport Beach. There are plenty of eager and desperate divorced women there," I said.

"Eager + desperate + divorced is the perfect combination for a woman. I'll see you there," the Devil replied with a sly wink.

I got into my car and drove to the exit to pay the parking lot attendant. I reached into my back pocket for my wallet and felt that it wasn't there.

A deep, empty yearning gripped my insides and everything I looked at seemed to have a dark yellow tint. I felt as if I were falling forward with my hands tied behind my back. My face would be crushed by the pavement at any moment—a sense of falling off a bridge into infinity. I was filled with a horrific swirl of emptiness, fear, dread, hopelessness and longing.

It was then that I realized that not just my wallet was

missing.

One Whiskey, Please

ZEKE SQUINTED HARD into the midday sun as his forehead soaked the brim of his hat with gritty sweat. His knees ached as they gripped the ribs of his white and brown horse. He should have been concerned with remaining incognito and surviving. But just one thing filled the entire landscape of his thoughts on this particular afternoon—the working girls at the saloon up ahead. Or as Vincent Van Gogh called them—*THE WOMEN WHO LOVE SO MUCH.*

He sure was fond of blondes, but brunettes had something special to offer too. Blonde or brunette? He would be forced to decide soon, as his horse was pacing with just a small bit of remaining dignity up to the Treasure Saloon.

* * *

After spending countless hours inching across the mercilessly bright desert, the interior of the Treasure Saloon looked about as dark as an ancient Egyptian sky at midnight. Zeke paced toward the bar with a wooden box tucked securely under his right arm—the contents knocking around clumsily inside.

"One whiskey please," said Zeke to the bar keeper, placing the box atop the bar.

"Whiskey's 20 cents, friend. It's a bit early, but some of the ladies upstairs might be ready for a go around. Most of 'em might still be sleeping off the laudanum. Cost you a dollar a hump," said the bar keeper, eyeing the rooms on the second floor.

"I'll just enjoy my whiskey for now, if you don't mind," responded Zeke.

Zeke didn't care for being rushed to the ladies. He would go upstairs and "hump" when he was good and ready.

The whiskey went down fast and smooth and tasted like liquid gold from the gods. Zeke belched under his breath and motioned with his hand to the bar keeper for another.

Zeke stared across the bar and saw a tall, fat man drinking alone. The Big Man had his hat politely placed on top of the bar, exposing his white bald head. He looked like a giant circus baby with no hair, a dark mustache, and a confused, leathery face.

The Big Man was gazing the other direction but Zeke had a strange and definite feeling that the Big Man had been looking straight at him just a moment before.

Zeke reached for the box slowly and placed one hand on top. Exactly 13 gold nuggets rested inside. Zeke had been assigned to deliver this and a few other packages to El Paso. The packages never made it to their intended destinations, and Zeke had become squarely focused on reaching his brother's ranch in Arizona Territory.

Zeke had not made the clean getaway he had hoped for. He should have known that such a large hunk of stolen gold would attract the worst type of bounty hunter. The kind who would demolish anything standing between him and his payday, without regard for women, children, or the infirm.

"I'll head upstairs now for some company," Zeke said to the bar keeper. He tucked the box under his arm and made his way toward the staircase, moving in an awkward and unconvincingly calm manner.

"Ladies, freshen up and make yourselves look pretty. A fella's making his way upstairs now and expects a good time," hollered the bar keeper. "Remember, a dollar a hump. Pay the lady in advance," the bar keeper added.

Zeke was forced to turn his back to the Big Man as he took his first steps up the staircase. He grazed the palm of his left hand gently over the butt of his holstered Colt Peacemaker to assure himself it was still there to protect him. It was there.

A portly blonde gal peaked her head out of the first room at the top of the stairs and greeted Zeke with a forced, nauseous smile. Zeke quickly stepped inside, paid the blonde gal a dollar, and said SHHHH!

The Big Man sauntered from the bar and slowly ascended the staircase. His meaty hand caressed the revolver dangling from his hip.

Zeke's eye peaked through a narrowly cracked door and watched the Big Man rise up the stairs. His heart thumped erratically and his armpits soaked his torso down to his ribs.

The Big Man reached the top step, stopped, and spied Zeke's gazing eye. Zeke's breathing stopped. He thrust the Peacemaker's long barrel through the door's narrow opening.

CRACK!!

Zeke's Peacemaker fired straight and true. At first, the Big Man winced as if he had just stubbed his toe on a nightstand in the middle of the night. He then howled and clawed at his left thigh. The bullet had severed the femoral artery and the Big Man looked like he was pissing blood, leaving a red puddle on the wooden floor.

Zeke zipped past the Big Man like a dragonfly and flew down the stairs—the box of stolen gold affectionately tucked under his arm.

Zeke busted through the saloon doors as if running from a nightmare. He clumsily hopped on his horse. "Let's go old girl," said Zeke, as he dug a spur into the horse's ribs. The horse shot through town and into the horizon like an apparition.

Arizona Territory was two days away. Zeke might make it if his horse held up, and if no one else was trailing him. A good meal, a hot bath, and family would be there to greet him. The working girls would have to wait.

They Are Here Now

THE LANDSCAPE of the Mojave Desert is beautiful, especially in the lonely blackness of midnight.

Winter's unforgiving, harsh wind seized me by the hair as a lied in bed. Nature's great outdoors became a part of my bedroom in an instant. I was sleeping, but not really. The lights were brighter than anything I had ever imagined and I wondered if looking straight at them would blind me forever.

I had heard the stories and read the newspaper articles and seen the movies. During early morning walks with my basset hound, Michael, lights would hover, twist, and sputter about in unusual patterns. Sometimes I would stop in my boots and give a slack-jawed stare, while Michael peed on the tan desert earth and rummaged for the bones of God's dead little forgotten creatures.

Those lights—they could not be explained by anything rational or scientific. The brightness would vanish as swiftly as it would appear. I hoped the visitors would be kind to us. But I have learned in life that if you have to hope really hard for something, things probably are not going to turn out well for you.

When the blinding bright lights invaded my reality, I was relieved to see that the visitors had finally arrived. Sometimes the waiting and worrying is worse than the eventual suffering. The wind was so cold and harsh that all I could do was cuddle in my blanket and close my eyes tight.

Maybe they'll take me home with them and make me their little Earthling mascot, and trot me out for intergalactic holidays and show me off as a trophy to make all their space buddies jealous.

The wind stopped and the lights dimmed. The face staring at me was recognizable. Large, oval, black eyes, with a tiny mouth. No nose. Except that this fellow had liquid skin. If you were to touch his head, your hand would go right through, yet the head and face somehow held together nice and sturdy.

The walls of my house disappeared. The visitors were standing at my bedside, examining me. I felt intense pressure around my skull, as if life itself was being manually squeezed from my head. Tremendous pulling and twisting at my legs made me scream in agony. As soon as I opened my mouth, the fellow with the black eyes seized my tongue and peeled off the top layer of skin. Then, all of my top teeth were extracted in a single, horrible yank.

More than anything, the visitors were enamored with my fingernails and toenails. All twenty nails were ripped from my body in an instant. I screamed like I had never screamed before, but they couldn't hear me. No ears.

I lied on my bed, shivering, crying, and screaming, wrapped in my brown fleece comforter. The fellow with the black eyes and liquid skin gently placed a single hand with long bony fingers atop my head, like a priest absolving a believer of his sins at mass. The pain disappeared in an instant and I felt euphoric.

Blackness overtook the light, the wind stopped, and the air became warm again. The walls returned to their designated places.

I looked to the floor and saw that Michael was sprawled out—half on his doggie bed and half on the Persian rug, with his basset hound ears spread eagle. His mouth was open slightly, with his tongue sticking out. He was fine.

The Writer

STEPHEN KING was once asked how he wrote so many amazing stories. His response was *"one word at a time."* King may be a sincere individual, but I have often suspected that he was taunting me directly with that quote. What an asshole.

I wish it were that easy—one word at a time. I have spent day after boring day in the public library and all I have come up with is the title "JAMIE'S WILD RIDE." It's not exactly a unique title, but at least it provides me with a jumping off point.

What I want more than anything in life is to be a great writer. No, a magnificent writer. But I learned at a young age that what I want and what I have are like third cousins twice removed who have never met one another. So, I sit and wait for inspiration to strike. I hand write a line or two on a yellow legal pad, then I quickly cross out what I have written. The fancy black and gold Mont Blanc pen I bought for myself has not helped one bit. Nor have I gained any inspiration from countless writing seminars hosted by pretentious academic pricks wearing turtlenecks.

The lion's share of my day is spent daydreaming about all sorts of things, including being a fantastic and famous writer.

But when I use the term "daydreaming," it would probably be more accurate if I said my mind was "sprint-dreaming." Because that's what it is—sprinting from one unrelated idea to the next without focus or order of any kind. One minute I am fascinating myself with a 20-year-old newspaper article I read about shark attacks in Florida, the next minute I am completely fixated on how many miles I can expect to get out of a new set of Goodyear tires.

I'm going to stand up from the library table now, and take a walk around the block. It's nighttime, and the library is almost empty, so no one will steal my yellow notepad. I will carry my black and gold Mont Blanc pen with me in my pocket just to be safe. There was a suspicious looking character at the north end of the library earlier this afternoon, and I think he had his eye on my pen. He was wearing a dark trench coat with military boots, and he had not shaved for several days. The man may have been mumbling something to himself, but I could not tell. His eyes were squinty and old, and he walked with an exhausted shuffle.

Also, the front desk librarian has been shooting uncanny glances my way and I think she is whispering to the other librarians about me. The librarian wears black horn-rimmed glasses and her hair is a brown sloppy mess with a pencil stuck through it in an unfashionable manner. I have seen her pacing the halls in her long flowery Woodstock skirt and black Doc Martens, re-shelving books. Who wears Doc Martens anymore?

The librarian keeps spying on me from the corner of her eye. I don't like her.

I'm walking down the middle of the street now and I'm feeling hot. I bump my head into something. I can't tell what it is, so I keep walking. I take off my blue t-shirt and toss it into the bushes because there is nothing wrong with a man walking shirtless in the heat of the summer. I'm still hot after removing my shirt, though, so I strip off my 501 Levi's (they never go out of style) and my underwear too. I'm still wearing my purple Converse All-Stars and white socks though, so technically I'm not naked. It is a hot, sweaty night, and there is no breeze. I will make my own breeze by running. I'm running now and the breeze against my chest and legs does not cool me off one bit. I have not showered for three days, and I can smell myself. The last time I took a shower I felt contaminants in the water, so I thought it best to skip showers for just a little while.

Cars are starting to honk their horns. I don't think they are honking at me, although it is possible since I am running in the middle of the road nearly naked. I run past a row of car dealerships with shiny reflective windows in front of the showrooms. Each time I glance at the car dealerships, I see a reflection of a naked man wearing only purple Converse and white socks running, with blood covering his face and chest. The blood is not just covering the man but is drip drip dripping onto his body like a gentle red waterfall. I can't figure out how this man found his way into the car dealerships without clothes, or how he runs inside the glass. He looks like me, but I know he must be someone else because I am a faster runner than him. I am also much more thin and muscular.

That old, familiar feeling returns to me. I am now viewing all the world as if peering through the dark green dirty water sloshing inside an old pickle jar. Every sight, sound, and physical sensation is tainted with muddy hopelessness and nausea. The sharp fangs of the dark green dirty pickle water fasten to my Adam's apple and won't let go. Then, the pestering voices start whispering the bad things that no one wants to hear.

The red and blue flashing lights are dim at first, then they become brighter as I continue to sprint toward the busy lights of downtown Newport Beach. It's them again. The men in the white coats. Yes, they still wear white coats after all these years. There will be two men, and they will both have incredibly strong hands like a couple of mountain gorillas. The two strong men at first will call me "Sir" as a courtesy, but their patience won't last long. The forced injection of Haldol will not just call me down but will make me forget who I am for a few days. That may be to my benefit because I don't want to be this person anymore.

After the Haldol wears off, I'll find a notepad and a pencil in the mental hospital, and I'll write something magnificent.

Five Year Commitment

IT IS BECOMING OBVIOUS to me that they do not like Americans here very much. I can tell by the way they look at me, and also because I am not making many friends. The food is horrible, the heat is brutal, and all I ever wanted was to be respected.

I was accepted as a French Foreign Legion cadet exactly two weeks ago today, and it has become clear that I have made a tremendous mistake.

* * *

After high school, there was not much going on. I decided to skip college because it all sounded so boring. Reading, writing and math would never be my cup of tea. But what I failed to understand at the time was that forgoing college would encapsulate me in a suburban nightmare—living with my parents, no parties, no girls and no concerts. Nothing remotely resembling fun. It was as if alien body snatchers stole all of the 18 and 19 year olds from my town during the three months following high school graduation.

I wasted my first year after high school delivering pizzas and working part-time as a telemarketer. I hung out with my few remaining slacker friends on Saturday nights at the local bowling alley. We would always manage to get our hands on some beer. Other than that, my hometown was completely dead.

A daytime TV commercial inspired me to make my way down to the Army recruiting station. I was greeted by a middle-aged soldier with a crisp, clean uniform and an incredibly unimaginative haircut. We chatted for a bit, and the soldier gave me some brochures. I then meandered a few blocks down the road, and had a similar conversation with a polite but intense gentleman at the Marines recruiting station. In the end, I never signed up for the U.S. Armed Forces. I don't really know why.

A few months later, I was perusing through a used bookstore, and happened upon a book about the French Foreign Legion. What surprised me most was that the Legion accepted cadets from any country in the world. Even better, the Legion would teach me how to speak French and would provide me with a new name and a French passport. I decided right away that my new name would be Rambo Norris.

Action, adventure, challenge—all of this awesomeness in an exotic location (France would seem exotic to you too if you grew up in Wisconsin). As a bonus, I was certain that the French women would be unbelievably hot and that they would go wild for my cool uniform and American accent.

* * *

You can only apply for the French Foreign Legion in person, in France. I squirreled away $3,000 working mind numbing jobs while living at home with my parents, then I secretly bought a one-way ticket to Paris.

As soon as I exited the plane, a pack of 50 muscular men in military fatigues ran by us civilians. A young French woman leaned into my ear and gently whispered *"French Foreign Legion."* Yes, the young woman was hot. I thought at that moment that I had made the best decision of my life. Little did I know what was in store for me.

* * *

Within four hours of my arrival in France, I was standing at the front of an unassuming, rundown building that was a French Foreign Legion recruiting center. I forcibly knocked three times. About 60 seconds passed before a tall, thin man with dark hair and beard stubble answered the door. The man motioned curtly with his hand, and I sheepishly followed him inside.

After about three days of testing and evaluation, I was informed that I had been accepted as a cadet. I signed a contract committing myself to five years of service. It was the first contract I had ever signed. I was eventually presented with

THEY ARE HERE NOW

my new name—Luc Bernard. So much for Rambo Norris.

The training is harsh and brutal and there is almost no rest. The marching and drills never end. I answer to a Corporal who is downright cruel, and the men do not respect him. When a cadet fails to perform drills correctly, the Corporal will hold out his arm straight and make a fist. The man is then ordered to run head on into it, smashing his own face. So completely dumb and pointless.

Some of the toughest and most determined people I have ever met are in the Legion. But I have also learned that the Legion is a good place for those who do not want to be burdened with the weight of thinking for themselves. If I succeed with my cadet training, my role as a Legionnaire will be to protect France's interests in Africa and elsewhere around the globe. What a waste of my youth.

I recently befriended "Pierre" (his new name). Pierre has red hair, light-skin, and freckles. What's funny is that Pierre is from Morocco and does not speak a lick of English. He reminds me of Ralph Malph from that old TV show, "Happy Days." Despite our language barrier, I have managed to speak with Pierre a little. It seems that Morocco is quite a bad place, and Pierre is glad to be here.

As for me, I miss going to the movies, eating pizza and Doritos, and seeing my family. There is another cadet here, a British boy just out of high school, who shares my dissatisfaction with the Legion and is ready to return to a country with a Queen. We have decided to desert at the first opportunity.

I have no money and no provisions. I am not sure what the penalty is for deserting the French Foreign Legion, but it is a risk I am willing to take. After two weeks of this misery, Saturday nights at the bowling alley drinking stolen beer with my loser friends sounds like paradise.

Steely, Crystal, and Me

UNLESS YOU ARE an aficionado of antiques and mechanical oddities, you may be unfamiliar with automatons. They look like mannequins without a soul, but they have plenty of character once you get to know them. And let me tell you, they have needs just like you and me. I don't mean that they get hungry, or that they have to pee every few hours, but they get jealous and suspicious, sometimes for no reason at all. And boy, are they intuitive. I learned all this the hard way, but we'll get to that later.

The first automaton appeared in our fine little shop sometime around 2010. To me, it looked like nothing more than metal, bolts, pulleys, and springs. It was actually quite a soulless creation—something straight out of a world with no rubber, wood, or dirt. I would catch the automaton staring at me with its creepy eyes and its puny, uninspiring appendages, like some sort of dead mannequin that never got a chance to stumble through machine puberty.

Despite its unimpressive design, I decided that the automaton deserved a name. I called it Steely, not so much because it was made of metal, but because its clean lines and cold resolve reminded me of those old Steely Dan recordings from the 1980s.

I have a long history of hearing things. I don't mean that I am schizophrenic or anything like that, but sometimes my mind races so fast that the thoughts jumble together to create voices telling me things. That's why when I heard Steely mumble *"I hate people who cruise through our shop and just browse around without buying anything,"* I just assumed it was my miserable mind racing itself into a big hot mess. Then I heard the clanking—Steely's arms jerking to and fro. As Steely turned toward me, small plates of metal shifted up and down as words dribbled from his mouth. Steely and I chatted and laughed it up quite a bit during that first summer. Automatons have quite a sense of humor once you get to know them well.

* * *

I've been employed at Once Bitten, Twice Shy Antiques since the summer of 1994. The gig was supposed to be temporary, but my ass has been sitting on the same metal stool behind the same counter for the past 25 years, so I don't suppose there will be any groundbreaking career changes in my life anytime soon. I never had plans to stay working at this old tired store for so long, but sometimes a man just doesn't have the juice to go out and meet new folks and carry on with all the jawboning and butt smooching required to move himself up the corporate ladder.

There is a burger joint next door to Once Bitten, and they serve just about the best double cheeseburgers and waffle cut fries I've ever laid my taste buds on. I'm quite a creature of habit, and I've been eating the same thing for lunch at that burger shop almost every day at noon sharp for more than 20 years.

A few years back, I strolled into the burger joint at noon, when I noticed this cute little honey of a waitress. She had wild, explosive curly red hair and an ass so firm that it made me a true believer in Jesus right there on the spot. Every day she would bring me my double bacon cheeseburger and waffle fries and a strawberry milkshake, always with a smile. Sometimes she'd even throw me a wink for good measure. When she would wink at me, I'd get all twinkly inside, like the time Susie Blum gave me a Valentine note covered with cute hand drawn hearts in the fourth grade.

I thought if I could muster up the courage to ask that mystery gal on a date, we might end up having a brood of kids together. Maybe we would even buy one of those pitiful hairless cats that look like they were created in the image of Freddy Krueger. In life, you never know what's lying in wait for you around the corner.

* * *

As it turns out, I am not so gutless after all. I eventually scraped together the courage to ask the waitress out on a date (her name is Crystal, by the way). Well, I can't exactly say that I gathered the courage all on my own. Steely could tell that I was distraught when I returned to the shop after lunch on weekdays. One day he said *"Jake, stop being a tomato can and ask that girl on a date. She's just a waitress for Christ sake, not the Duchess of Orange County. She's probably used to being hit on by creeps all day long, and she'll be interested in you, unless you act like a nervous loser and wet yourself."*

Crystal and I dated for a while and eventually I fell in love with her. Whether she fell in love with me, I don't know. Perhaps she took pity on me or maybe she decided that at the age of 32, she was becoming a bit long in the tooth and had to accept the best thing that came her way, which luckily was me. Sometimes a woman just likes to go to work on a man, like a fixer-upper that she can try to mold however she sees fit. The heart of a woman is a mysterious thing which I quit trying to understand many moons ago.

I eventually asked Crystal to marry me and she said yes. We were married in a small ceremony on Catalina Island in 2012. Whether she got the better end of the bargain or whether I did, I still don't know. I know what I'm supposed to say: *I'm just a big dummy and I'm lucky that she married me.* But what I really think is that it is hard for women out there. If a woman can find a man whose pecker works and who is in good shape and who is not a drunk and who makes a decent living and does not cheat on her, said woman has found a treasure more rare than the Hope Diamond.

Our marriage started out just fine, while it was just the two of us.

* * *

Crystal turned out to be a damn good wife. For starters, she was an exceptional conversationalist with a fine ear for jazz. After work, we would hang out at home, reading books and listening to Oscar Peterson and Stan Getz records. Her taste in books was more highbrow than mine—David Foster Wallace and the like. She tried to give me the hard sell about what a genius Wallace was, but I just didn't get it. You could give Wallace an outline to write The Great Gatsby, and he'd find a way to muck it up by writing a 25 page paragraph obsessing over the color and texture of a chauffeur's sport coat.

To her credit, Crystal never looked down her nose at me when I would embark on one of my Stephen King marathons. I liked to start with the classics like It and Christine, then work my way through more recent goodies from King's mind. Crystal once said "horror is like pornography," but maybe she didn't mean that in a bad way.

Of course I never told Crystal about my frequent conversations with Steely. But she knew that I was fond of him, so she surprised me on our first wedding anniversary by buying Steely and bringing him home. At first, he was placed in the corner of our living room by the fireplace, but he looked so lonely there that I convinced Crystal to move him into the den so he could be with us when we ate our meals and when I drank my coffee and read the newspaper on Sunday mornings.

After Crystal would go to bed, I'd stay up late chatting with

Steely. Sometimes we'd talk and talk and I'd drink coffee all night long until the sun slowly painted the cold sky orange.

As an only child I led somewhat of a lonely existence and didn't have many friends. Just a lot of Three's Company and Twilight Zone reruns to keep me company on quiet weekday afternoons. Steely's companionship meant a lot to me, and I never forgot how he gave me the confidence to ask Crystal on that first date. Steely was making a nice place for himself in our cozy home.

Sometimes Crystal would wind up Steely and pull his levers and we would sit together and watch him do his little routine and we would add ridiculous dialogue to his unhuman movements. *Excuse me, someone told me this is where to sign up to join the Coast Guard. Pardon me, do you have any Grey Poupon?*

I never confided in Crystal about my conversations with Steely. There is only so much a man can share about himself within the confines of a marriage before he crosses a fine line and risks the possibility of his wife thinking he is a bona fide looney bird. As far as Crystal was concerned, Steely was just an antique from another era that had captured my imagination.

Despite my marital bliss with Crystal, I sensed Steely was not overly pleased about our home life. On many occasions, I caught him shooting wicked glances toward Crystal. When Crystal would cook eggs at the stove in the morning, Steely would slightly turn his head and glare so intensely at Crystal's back that I was afraid he would burn a hole straight through her spine. One time, I saw Steely swipe his arm over the kitchen counter, spilling vegetable oil all over the linoleum floor. Crystal came walking through the kitchen and her foot slid over the oil. A tiny yelp shot from her throat, and down she went. She bruised her coccyx and was laid up for about a week, but things could have been much worse.

I told Steely not to worry—we would make time to hang out and watch the Rams knock the sass out of the Saints on Sunday. But Steely didn't want to hear it. He just stood in the corner with his cold arms hanging stiffly at his sides, refusing to talk. An upset wife who does not want to talk is one thing, but an angry, unpredictable automation that no longer wishes to speak is uncharted territory.

* * *

Last Saturday around midnight, I rolled out of bed and stumbled down the hallway to relieve myself in the bathroom. I used to hang out at the beach with my teenage buddies, making fun of old men and their unending parade of physical complaints. *Oh, my back hurts—ouch, my knees don't bend anymore—my knuckles are swollen!* Now here I am, a middle aged geezer with an enlarged prostate, peeing four times a night and greeting each morning with urine stains splattered across the front of my pajama bottoms. Father time is one heartless son of a bitch.

Crystal always liked to keep a night light on in our

bedroom so we could see where we were walking in the dark. I stepped through the doorway to return to bed and sternly planted my feet on the carpet. At first, I was not sure what I was seeing. There was a glistening, shiny object covering Crystal's side of the bed. I could see her legs near the foot of the bed, but everything from her waist up was out of view. I took two tentative steps closer and saw things a little bit better, but nothing made sense. Then I heard the whispering.

Steely was smothering Crystal, with his right forearm over her chest and his left hand cradling the side of her head. Crystal slowly turned her head toward me, and I witnessed pure terror blossoming within her damp eyes. Steely was whispering softly into her right ear, as his left hand lovingly caressed the side of her head. I could not hear what he was saying, but with each new jumble of words, Crystal's eyes grew larger and larger, until they developed a hysterical glow. Steely kept talking for a few minutes, and I just stood there as frozen as a tundra night.

I saw Crystal's abdomen slowly rise. Her mouth opened, and she unleashed the most piercing, deafening scream I had ever heard. Steely rolled over and Crystal got out of bed and walked straight past me. I put out my arm and tried to stop her, but she placed her index finger over my lips, stared deep into my brain, then kept walking toward the garage. Crystal grabbed the keys to her Camaro IROC off the little hook attached to the wooden pig by our front door, paced barefoot down the driveway wearing her light blue nightgown, started the IROC, and drove down the dark street slower than a valet parking attendant. Steely and I stood on the sidewalk in front of my house, watching the IROC sweep Crystal out of our lives forever.

* * *

I never did ask Steely what he said to Crystal. I suppose I should have done more to try to stop her from leaving. I suppose I should have prevented Steely from turning into the ruler of our little house. I suppose I should have been a better listener when Crystal tried to talk to me after work.

But that's all over now. It's just me and Steely in our bachelor pad. Nothing but nachos, hot dogs, ice cold Guinness, Chuck Norris movies, and football all day on Sundays. This weekend the Saints clobbered the Rams in a shutout, 35–0.

Hitchhiker on a Rainy Night

HEY THERE, thanks for picking me up. I was starting to wonder whether anyone could see me standing on the side of the highway with my pathetic dirty white thumb pointing up toward the moon. Deep down, most people know hitchhikers are harmless. Those old wives tales about hitchhikers abducting and killing innocent drivers are just excuses for people to be selfish and keep driving down the road, when some unlucky fella like myself needs a lift. But I suppose my long wet hair and old beat up Levi's jacket don't make me look like a member of the Mormon Tabernacle choir, huh?

Oh, howdy kids. I almost didn't see your two kids strapped in those car seats in the back. Looks like your baby girl is conked out and catching some serious ZZZZZZs. I guess these days, it's all about safety this and safety that. They say kids are the future, and I suppose that's right, but there's an awful lot of overkill when it comes to ensuring the safety of youngsters. When I was a kid, I rode my motorcycle all over town without a helmet, and no one cared two hoots. My old man used to plop my butt on a case of Pabst Blue Ribbon in the back seat. That was his idea of a booster seat. Hell, your two kids look like they're strapped in good and tight with those three buckle harnesses, ready to race a few laps in the Indianapolis 500!

Where are you headed with those two little beauties in the backseat? Cool! I bet the kids will love Las Vegas—there's a lot for the youngsters to do there these days. I don't need a ride all the way to Vegas, but if you could take me about 70 miles up the road to Barstow, that would be boss. I don't think they'll find me if I can just make it to Barstow.

You see, I'd been a patient at Bay View Mental Hospital for some time. It's funny, that name. I can tell you firsthand there ain't no bay and there ain't no view in that dump. For the first eight months of my "stay" at the luxurious Bay View facility, I had twice a week visits with this sweetie of a gal named Dr. Nicholson. I was pretty sure Dr. Nicholson had the hots for me, but she couldn't let on as she was trying to keep things professional. I respected her for that, but sometimes you've got to be the man and make a move when a lady keeps making bedroom eyes at you. During one of our sessions, Dr. Nicholson told me that we had made a "breakthrough," as she put it. So I reached across to her, nice and slow, and gently squeezed her thigh. I was real gentlemanly about it, though.

The next thing I know, I show up for my next session two days later, and it was goodbye beautiful Dr. Nicholson and hello hairy old man Dr. Patterson. So I sat there across from Dr. Patterson, staring at his tired old eyes and stale salt-and-pepper beard and thrift store green grandpa sweater. Dr. Patterson droned on about this medication and that medication, trying to formulate some sort of zombie cocktail that could slither down my gullet.

Early this morning, I palmed a knife from the dining hall and escaped through the food storage warehouse. Adios Dr. Patterson and all you bastards at the zombie mill!

I had never hitch hiked before, but as I was standing out there in the rain I couldn't help but think of one of my favorite horror movies from the 1980s: THE HITCHER, with C. Thomas Howell. Have you ever seen that one? What, never? Oh man, you're missing out! C. Thomas Howell is this young kid driving down a deserted highway, when he picks up a bad ass hitchhiker played by Rutger Hauer. The hitchhiker is an absolute psycho, and at one point he pulls out a knife and sticks it right up to the eye of the driver, and asks him if he knows how much blood would shoot out of his eye if he were to poke it with the knife. The teenage driver is a great big sissy, and all he can do is stutter and stammer while the hitchhiker confidently and calmly waves that shiny blade next to his eyeball and up and down his cheek.

If the driver had been any kind of a man he would've taken that knife and rammed it right into the hitchhiker's you know where. But instead, he hesitated like a cowardly little schoolboy and probably wet himself, while the hitchhiker remained in full control of the situation. The driver finds himself in a big mess of trouble with the hitchhiker later in the movie, but I won't spoil the ending for you. I must say that you look a helluva lot tougher than the colossal wimp driver in The Hitcher.

Check out this knife I swiped from the kitchen before I skedaddled out of Bay View. I think we've developed a pretty good rapport, and you should trust me by now. Let's do a little recreation from The Hitcher to help pass the time along this dull stretch of highway. It'll be just like the movie! In The Hitcher, the hitchhiker slowly lifted the shiny blade right up to the driver's eye, just like this, then he said something like: *"Say kid, how much blood do you think would squirt out of your eye if I were to jam this knife into your eyeball?"*

Do you think your kids would wake up before your car swerved, flipped, and then rolled off the highway?

Are you seriously starting to sweat? Even in the dark, I can see drops of sweat trickling down your sideburns, onto your neck. LOL, what a total wuss you turned out to be.

Hey, wait a minute. I was just joking. Let go of my arm, man!!!

* * *

BARSTOW TRIBUNE
UNIDENTIFIED MAN FOUND DEAD ON INTERSTATE 15
February 10, 2019
By Jedidiah Watson

A man was found dead early Wednesday morning, lying along the side of Interstate 15, approximately 20 miles south of Barstow. The man's throat had been slit from ear to ear, and a kitchen knife had been inserted straight through his right eye, into his brain. The unidentified man appeared to be approximately 25 years of age, with long brown hair. He was wearing a dark blue Levi's jacket.

Anyone with information regarding the identity of this man is asked to please contact investigator Murdoch Pupkin at (555) 555–7725.

Deciding on a Loaf of Bread

STAY FOCUSED and this won't take long. I just need to pick up a loaf of whole wheat bread at the store.

Has the World Series started yet? I hate baseball. People who drone on and on about baseball are so boring.

Concentrate on how the ground feels below my feet. I am wearing sandals and my toes feel cool in the night's autumn breeze.

I think I have an ingrown toenail. My left big toe looked red and puffy this morning. I hope the ingrown toenail does not become infected with MRSA, then they'll have to amputate my foot.

Take another step and focus on your breathing—the way the air feels entering the nose and exiting the mouth. The bread should be in aisle five, next to the ice cream aisle. Maybe I can pick up some ice cream and we can make banana splits for dessert tonight.

The ringing in my ears won't go away. Maybe I have a brain tumor that's putting pressure on the nerves next to my ears, causing that ringing sound. I hope the ringing doesn't become so bad that I eventually become deaf. It would be really hard to use sign language every day because I have carpal tunnel at both wrists.

Keep taking deep breaths, and keep walking. There are so many damn choices for bread! But it's okay, I already decided in advance what I want—the hefty whole-grain wheat bread that tastes like dry tree bark but is apparently good for you. OK, now that I've got the bread, I'll just scoot on down to the ice cream aisle. Neapolitan sounds good for tonight.

It's freezing in the ice cream aisle! I hope I don't get frostbite on my fingers carrying the half-gallon of ice cream to the checkout counter. I'll bet it's less than 75 steps from the ice cream aisle to the checkout stand. I'll start counting now...1, 2, 3... If I'm wrong, and it's more than 75 steps, is that an omen that I'll be diagnosed with cancer before the end of the year?

The air feels cool when it floats past my sinuses and finds a temporary home in my lungs. The air becomes soothing and warm by the time it exits my body through my lips.

The checkout girl looks homely and bored. That's probably because she can tell by looking at me that I'm boring. I am adding nothing to her dull day. I shouldn't shop at this store anymore. I wonder if she has a cat. I'm allergic to cats.

This last part is easy. I just need to remove my wallet from my pocket, grab the credit card, stick the chip into the little machine, then press "OK." Then I'm out of here.

Checkout stands are filthy places. Germs galore. If I get

sick I'm not going to the doctor because there are even more disgusting germs at the doctor's office. And medical malpractice kills more people each year than shark attacks, tornadoes, and hurricanes combined. I'm going to surf in the morning. If a shark tries to eat me, I probably won't put up a fight.

That wasn't so bad. I successfully purchased a loaf of bread. I even managed a vague smile and a little wink toward the homely cashier girl.

Tomorrow's a new day.

Zeke Aims High

BY THE TIME Zeke was able to savor his first slug of whiskey, the mercury had mightily inched its way past the 100° mark. Zeke found a nice shady place for his horse, Darla, around back, with plenty of water. He then strutted through the swinging doors of the Sassy Susan Saloon.

* * *

Zeke would have never survived without Darla. She had carried him through the Mojave Desert and straight into Arizona territory more than once. Darla was a loyal, good old horse who always seemed to appreciate Zeke's stories around the campfire after supper. When a man's riding alone mile after sun drenched mile, his horse is the only soul on the planet who will listen politely to his bitching and moaning without raising so much as a hoof in protest.

Not long after President McKinley's assassination, Zeke caught himself a nasty case of Montezuma's revenge down in Mexico. The water was so cool and refreshing going down, but oh so evil coming out. He had been too sick to sit up on Darla, so he hunched himself forward, feebly hugged her neck, nestled his face into her long brown mane, and let Darla carry him clean out of Mexico and into Texas.

* * *

Zeke placed his wide brimmed leather hat upon the bar like a gentleman before enjoying his first drink. The Sassy Susan Saloon was not exactly the classiest of joints, but that was just fine because Zeke was not in the mood for a whole lot of carrying on. He would enjoy exactly three shots of whiskey before making his acquaintance with a working girl upstairs. Zeke had it on good information that Beatrice was in town, hard at work at The Sassy Susan until the end of July. Zeke had learned through much trial and error that Beatrice was one of the few working girls worth returning to and tipping well. She really seemed to care.

Exactly three shots of whiskey, not four. Zeke knew from his youth that the fourth and fifth shots of whiskey made it so that his oil derrick did not work as it should when the moment with a beautiful young woman finally presented itself.

A tall, skinny man with a boney face and a pointy nose strutted into the Sassy Susan. His waist was so slender that his holster looked as if it were about to slip right off and go THUD! on the floor. Although there was an entire row of empty bar stools, the skinny man sat right next to Zeke. So close that their elbows were almost rubbing.

"Hey fella, you happen to see that mangy old brown and white horse out back? That's gotta be about the most pathetic looking, ugly damn horse I've ever seen," said the skinny man.

Zeke suddenly noticed his face getting physically hot. Both of his hands suddenly turned themselves into tight fists. Zeke must have been staring at the skinny man with his eyes bulging out of his head, because the skinny man turned to him and asked "What in the hell's the matter with you, friend?"

"You and me, outside, right now you dirty son of the bitch," hollered Zeke.

"Hold it right there, partner. If that old brown horse is yours, I didn't mean no offense. It's just that your horse is so god awful ugly and beaten up, she looks like she's seen better days, that's all. Hell, I got a real nice horse I'll sell you if you're interested," said the skinny man.

Zeke stared at the man for a few seconds, trying to figure out if he was serious, if he was joking, or if he was just a complete idiot. After giving it some thought, Zeke decided that it didn't matter which category the skinny man fell into. The skinny man was going to meet Zeke in the street, and that was that.

"Outside, now!" yelled Zeke, his face bright red.

* * *

The mercilessly intense sun struck Zeke in the face in a way that made him feel as if God were punishing him for some bad act many years past. Boot leather cradled his feet tightly as he stepped toward the center of the dusty road. The whiskey swam through Zeke's head and made him feel uninhibited and confident.

The skinny man followed Zeke toward the center of the dusty road, where they met face to face.

"Let's stand back to back, then take 10 paces. After 10 paces, turn and fire," said Zeke.

"You got it, pal," said the skinny man with a shaky voice.

Zeke gently glided his fingers over his right hip, feeling the soothing, cold steel of his Colt Peacemaker. Zeke heard the skinny man take his first step away from him, so Zeke took his first step. With each step, Zeke's heart raced faster and faster. His temples were throbbing with savage viciousness. Zeke's jaw clenched tight, and he felt as if he were grinding his molars into fluffy white powder.

At step number six, Zeke managed a swift glance over his shoulder. The skinny man had his right hand on his pistol and was slowly turning to face Zeke, like a sly old hound dog quietly swiping a slice of roast beef from the dinner table.

THAT DIRTY, CHEATING SON OF A BITCH!

Zeke slapped his right hand on the Colt Peacemaker. The handle fit the palm of his hand better than any custom leather glove. Zeke spun around with his leather boots squarely planted exactly 18 inches apart and with his head and chest directly facing the skinny man. His right hand steadily pointed the Peacemaker directly at the skinny man.

Zeke remembered what happened to poor old Garth, his friend from Tucson. He got overexcited in a duel and pulled the trigger too early, shooting himself in the thigh. Garth bled to death in less than ten minutes.

AIM HIGH. SHOOT THIS TALL SKINNY BASTARD RIGHT BETWEEN THE EYES AND BLOW THE TOP OF HIS SKULL CLEAR INTO MEXICO. TAKE A DEEP BREATH, AND DON'T SHOOT UNTIL YOUR AIM IS STRAIGHT AND TRUE.

Zeke felt pressure on his right index finger. His Peacemaker kicked back with a vengeance. Smoke casually floated from the barrel. Zeke heard the gunshot, but it sounded as if it were miles away. Just as Zeke shot, he saw an orange flash from the right hand of the skinny man.

WE FIRED AT THE SAME TIME. DID WE BOTH MISS?

A fountain of bright red blood suddenly shot from the top of the skinny man's head, with brown chunks soaring through the dusty hot air. It reminded Zeke of a Fourth of July firework that fired just a little, but was a dud. The skinny man's bones immediately collapsed onto themselves and he crumpled into a sad little heap in the middle of the dirt road. If Darla was watching, she was surely pleased.

Zeke noticed a sense of pressure and fullness at his left foot. He looked down and saw that his boot was quickly transforming into a pathetic crimson swamp. Zeke frantically took an inventory of his entire body, starting with his crotch. An incredible wave of relief cascaded over Zeke, as he realized that his oil derrick was as good as new.

A MAN'S GOT TEN TOES, BUT JUST ONE OIL DERRICK.

Zeke limped his way back into the Sassy Susan Saloon, where he tossed three gold pieces onto the bar and demanded a doctor, a hot bath, and Beatrice. All Zeke needed was a few bandages, a bottle of laudanum, and full dose of Beatrice's fine hospitality.

A Poodle Named Denise

THE HIGHWAY RUNNING from Orange County to Las Vegas is desolate. Nothing but light brown earth and bright blue skies expanding into infinity.

Jim and Judy were headed out to Vegas for one of those "rekindle the old flame" weekends that married couples take every now and again. After 27 years of marriage, Jim supposed it wasn't such a bad idea, even if Judy's sister had suggested it.

It's one thing to be married to the same person day in and day out. But sitting right next to that overly familiar person in a car for six hours straight, well, that's not for the faint of heart.

"Babe, I'm sorry but I just can't take any more Top 40. Can we listen to Howard Stern for a bit?" asked Jim, reaching for the radio dial.

"If I wanted to hear middle-aged windbags babble about tits and boners, I would hang around your buddies at the Elks Lodge," replied Judy.

"Oh for Christ's sake, loosen up honey. What happened to the old party animal that I married," said Jim, squeezing her knee.

"She had three kids and they sucked the will to live from

her tired soul. I've got to pee really bad. Pull over at the next rest stop," said Judy, squirming in her seat.

Jim turned the wheel and slowly pulled the car off the highway and into a parking stall.

"I hate rest stops, the bathrooms have piss all over the floor," said Jim.

"No use complaining. It's hot as hell in this miserable desert wasteland, so let's make it quick," said Judy.

* * *

There were a decent amount of cars in the parking lot, but Judy could not spy a single person.

About 100 feet ahead, between the men's and women's restroom, Judy spotted an old woman lying face down on the ground. The lady was wearing a light blue jogging suit with bright white running shoes. Her black leather purse was clutched in her right hand. Some of the contents had spilled onto the ground. The old woman was not moving.

Jim and Judy quickly walked toward the old woman's limp body. There was no other person in sight.

As Judy approached the woman, she heard a low, guttural growl echoing from the men's room. Judy stood bolt upright with her heart suddenly racing and her armpits sweating.

From the men's room entrance stepped very slowly a bright and fluffy white patch of fur. This toy poodle had bushy, sculpted fur at the legs, head, and ears like one of those ridiculous show dogs on T.V. She also had a pink collar with a shiny silver chain dangling carefree.

As the poodle made its way toward Judy, she noticed its professionally manicured toenails. But what really caught Jim and Judy's attention was the dark red patch of stained fur around the poodle's mouth and snout.

The poodle slowly inched her way closer, bearing her sharp little teeth and producing the deep growl of a pitbull. When Judy moved a bit closer to the woman to check for a pulse, the poodle grunted viciously, and drool spilled from her blood red mouth.

"Don't move toward that woman, Judy, that dog will attack you," said Jim.

Out of the corner of Jim's eye, he saw a young couple sprinting from the woman's room toward their car. The poodle quickly turned its little head with a bloody snarl. The marshmallow torpedo darted toward the couple—pink toenails tap dancing across the concrete.

The couple was no match for the poodle's speed. The man was wearing shorts, and the poodle sunk her teeth deep into his calf and barked shrilly. The man in shorts yelled profanities and kicked the poodle hard enough to make her lose interest. The couple hobbled to their car, while the poodle loyally returned to the old lady on the ground, and to Jim and Judy.

"My God, everyone must be hiding in the restrooms, scared to death of this tiny spawn of Satan," said Judy.

They stood there motionless next to the old lady, as the poodle stood ten feet away, shifting her stare from Jim to Judy, then back to the old lady.

Jim noticed from the corner of his eye that the old lady's feet were starting to twitch. Her eyes then started to flutter and her hands began clenching and releasing.

"She's coming to," said Jim.

The poodle's entire being jolted to attention like a new Marine in boot camp and her furry ears perked up. She licked the old lady's face over and over.

"Denise, Denise, is that you," said the old lady. "Oh Denise, my lovey-dovey-poopy-woopy-kins."

The old lady noticed Jim and Judy. "I must have had one of my episodes. This heat really gets to me now. I hope little Denise here didn't scare anyone too much. She can become a bit feisty when I faint. She's really a sweety pie, though," said the old lady.

"We're OK ma'am, but some other folks had a run in with your dog while you were out. Are you alright to drive?" asked Jim.

"Oh, I'm just fine, young man," said the old lady.

Jim and Judy shuffled back to their Volvo. Judy looked back and saw the old lady holding the poodle in her arms like a woolly baby. The poodle snuggled her stained muzzle deep into the old lady's bosom, with her tail hanging over the old lady's arm.

The remaining victims emerged from the restrooms and stumbled their way to their cars.

"What the hell just happened," said Jim, as he buckled his seat belt.

"An evil little pooch named Denise, now I've really seen it all," said Judy.

"The loyalty of a good dog is limitless," said Jim, as their Volvo rolled on down the highway.

Encounter at Dawn

THE FIRST THING JAY NOTICED was the bitter cold sand pressed against his bare feet. The sky was still dark and the full moon was white and glowing. A slight, cold breeze blew from the north, causing goose bumps on Jay's bare chest. Winter had arrived in Southern California.

Jay surfed only at dawn. His old eyes could no longer handle the harsh glare from the sun and his old temper couldn't handle crowds. As the sun began its ascent, Jay noticed a small rectangular sign stuck in the sand. *Shark Sighting January 16. Swim At Your Own Risk.*

Take off the clothes, slip on the wetsuit, put on the booties, pull the zipper, strap the leash around the ankle, rub wax on the board, insert ear plugs, stretch the arthritic joints. All set.

Jay walked toward the shoreline and looked as far north as he could. Not a single person in the water, just a few folks walking dogs along the beach. He then gazed south toward the pier and confirmed the water was empty in all directions. Just Jay.

The first steps into the water felt great, as his wetsuit provided warm protection. Jay shuffled into waist deep water, hopped on his board, and started paddling. He pushed his board down and dove under the first wave. His head instantly felt like a frozen block of ice.

Jay paddled back and forth for a bit to warm up, then sat up on his board and gazed into the horizon. There were good sized waves with bigger sets rolling in every five minutes or so. The tranquility of floating in the water and simply looking off into infinity was just fine, waves or no waves. A pelican flew by low and smooth, gently scraping its wing across the water.

The wind crafted hollow waves and Jay found himself in the middle of some nice open barrels within a few minutes. Soon, his arms started to feel rubbery. Time for a little rest.

Jay paddled beyond the waves and sat up on his board. Light was sneaking up and over the two-story houses which sat comfortably on the sand. The sun beamed bright on the jetties and made the rocks shine like wet marbles.

There was a slight chop in the water, but Jay knew exactly what he was seeing. At first it was just a small triangle calmly slicing along the top of the ocean surface. *Stay still, don't appear to be injured.* Jay remained still, but certainly not calm. About 15 feet separated Jay from the first pass of the small triangle.

The triangle then made a closer pass and was fully exposed, with a large gray torpedo confidently gliding just beneath. *That's almost a 20 footer.* Great Whites had been spotted up and down the coast for months. They only seem theoretical until there is one right in front of you.

The Great White slowly circled Jay like someone walking around a car at a dealership, carefully considering a purchase. *Circle, Circle, Circle.* Taking its time. Although he was scared, Jay had not given much thought to the possibility that he could actually be bitten. How could he be attacked by a shark when the sun was rising on a beautiful day and he had to be at work by 9:00?

The Great White drifted out, then started directly toward Jay's board. The head, eyes, and nose were visible now and incredibly lifelike. The tailfin stood out from the water as a formidable monument. The Great White charged at Jay and beat its tailfin back and forth, erupting water.

The time for sitting still was through. Jay lied on his board and began respectfully paddling toward shore. *Don't splash. Don't appear injured.* Feet straight up in the air, heart beating like a kick drum. Paddle, Paddle, Paddle. Eyes focused on the dry sandy shore and the beach houses sitting in a neat little row.

The Great White approached Jay's left side quickly. Jay's breath escaped and he could not scream. There was no sharp pain, but the pressure at Jay's left arm was intense and real. Jay saw the eyes of the Great White staring back at him honestly and intently. The teeth were halfway up Jay's bicep, anchored on tight. The Great White maneuvered its head back and forth, reminding Jay of a parent scolding a misbehaving child. Jay tried to pull away but the Great White's strength was truly superhuman. *This is really happening.*

Jay was most taken by the indifference of the Great White. It did not seem angry, curious, or even hungry. It was just there, latched to his body. There was no soundtrack, no suspense, no drama. Just fear, surprise, and a rendezvous with mortality.

The Great White's jaws slid down the left bicep and held firm at the elbow. Jay felt a "pop," and the pressure was gone. The Great White calmly disappeared into the blue depths.

Jay made his way to shore kicking and paddling with one arm. The blood was bright red but the water and sand were turning maroon and the blood was coming too fast. He lied on his back as the cold water gently splashed his feet and legs. A few more pelicans flew overhead as the sky turned bright periwinkle blue. Jay felt cold, calm and drowsy.

Jay was glad he had caught some amazing waves that morning. He remembered surfing with his pack of buddies in the blistering sun when he was 16. He thought of his first kiss on the beach underneath fireworks on the Fourth of July. Jay faded as he remembered all the surreal sunrises and sunsets. He thought of the Great White. He thought of the people he would miss. Jay was glad to belong to the ocean.

Violent Ones Make Great Pets

MY BOX TURTLE, Austin, is a good little fellow, but turtles do not make the best of companions.

An advertisement in the San Juan Capistrano Tribune caught my attention: *Pet Adoption, Sunday, 1 o'clock to 4 o'clock. Rescue a Pet, Save a Life.* I had never thought of myself as a particularly charitable person, but I thought if I could "Rescue" or "Save" a life, that would make me feel pretty darn good about myself.

I stumbled into Pet Depot half-asleep at around 2 o'clock on Sunday, October 1. I had been fighting a rough hangover from the night before. That whole "hair of the dog" thing is pure bullshit. Two more cans of Guinness at 10 AM just made me feel a whole lot worse.

A middle-aged woman wearing Wrangler jeans and running shoes and a red polo shirt with a name tag reading "Hi, I'm Suzanne," approached me.

"Hi, I'm Suzanne. Welcome to our little pet adoption shindig."

"I live alone with my pet turtle. His name is Austin," I blurted out.

"Oh, I just love turtles," replied Suzanne, politely.

"I'm looking for a nice dog or cat—something that doesn't shed too much," I said.

"Absolutely! We have dogs and cats of all sizes, all colors, and just about every breed you can imagine. Dogs and cats are wonderful companions, but have you ever considered an *alternative* type of pet?" asked Suzanne.

"What exactly is an 'alternative' pet," I asked.

"Well, it's kind of hard to explain. Follow me back here and I can show you what we've got. Come on, don't be bashful," said Suzanne, motioning with her arm.

The back of **Pet Depot** was dimly lit, with a dank feel. Way in the back next to the trash cans and discarded office furniture was a row of steel cages, about 15 feet x 15 feet. As I slowly approached, I noticed a perfumy type of smell. Or maybe it was cologne. Actually, now that I really think about it, it was a musk scent. Each cage had only one inhabitant, each with a unique appearance. Some were hefty, some were thin, some had hair, and some were bald. Some of them walked upright on two legs, and others walked on all fours. All of them were speaking understandable but broken English.

"These guys have been abandoned by their owners. They all need a good home. Don't worry, all of these cute little critters are retired from their violent ways," said Suzanne.

"Violent ways? What are these things?" I asked.

"That's not exactly easy to explain. These guys were found in an uninhabited section of the Brazilian Rainforest. They're not quite human, not quite animal. Some of them have human features and most of them are smart enough to speak limited English. Look at their fantastically bright neon colored hair— blue, green, and orange. They like to play rough, and they don't seem to know how strong they are. They tend to get a little hot under the collar, if you know what I mean. Temper tantrums galore! But deep down inside, they've got a lot of love to give. They just need someone who will be patient with them and steer them clear of their naturally violent tendencies. Some folks call them 'Violent Ones,' but I don't care for that term."

"This little gal here looks interesting. Can I see her?" I asked.

"Her name is Ursula. She likes eating pizza," said Suzanne.

Ursula stood on two stubby little feet, with the stiff and proud posture of an aristocrat. Her straight bright green hair casually tumbled over her shoulders, down to the middle of her back. Ursula had enormous black eyes that looked right through you like you weren't there. A mouthful of sharp, bright white teeth burst out of her face when she smiled. She looked young and physically fit, despite being stuck in a tiny cage at the back of Pet Depot day and night. Ursula was wearing a white T-shirt with a portrait of Charles Manson's creepy, crazed face splattered across the front.

Ursula slowly but confidently walked right up to me and said "I want go home now. Please take home and I be good. I get along with others and make nice. No more bad things I do.

Promise."

I don't know if it was her confidence or her straightforward manner, but whatever it was, Ursula was very believable.

"I think Ursula will make a fine pet. I'll take her."

* * *

The first few weeks at home were a bit of an adjustment for Ursula. She was good about eating my home cooking and using the bathroom. She did not make much of a mess, and seemed to enjoy being curled up on the couch watching Dukes of Hazard reruns.

And boy, does Ursula love movies. Her favorite is The Shining. She rapidly claps her hands with glee every time Jack Nicholson slams the ax straight into the heart of the cook at the Overlook Hotel. I get a bit concerned when she gets so excited about violence, but when she's happy, I'm happy.

I was shocked to come home from work one day to find Ursula with the dead rats. She was standing in the middle of the living room facing the front door, with a comically massive smile on her face and a blank stare in her dead black eyes. She was holding a dead rat in each hand, with both arms raised high and proud. Ursula grasped both dead rats by their tails and spun them around in a circular motion. Blood flinging from their tiny rat noses. She looked like one of those military helicopters with two propellers in the front, side by side. Ursula kept swinging those dead rat propellers around and around and around, all the while maintaining a frozen wide-eyed grin.

"Look at dead rat I find. I do good thing today," said Ursula.

I didn't give up, though. I kept working with Ursula and showing her the importance of caring for other creatures and being kind. The concepts of charity, kindness, and sharing seemed foreign and difficult for Ursula to understand. But she was making progress. She started feeding my turtle, Austin, while gently petting the top of his head. She even made friends with some of the neighborhood kids. I bought her a Razor scooter so she could ride up and down the sidewalk with them on weekday afternoons, after school let out.

* * *

Last night I was asleep, when I heard a thump at the foot of my bed. I put on my glasses, and saw Ursula standing there silently, holding a steak knife. She had a huge smile on her face. Her black eyes were rolled up into the back of her head, revealing just the whites of her eyes. Her bright green hair covered the sides of her face, spilling over her thin shoulders. The tip of the steak knife pointed straight at me like a spear.

I asked Ursula what she was doing, and she said that she just liked to watch me sleep. I asked her why she was holding the knife, and she told me that she liked to cut people. I slowly approached Ursula and removed the knife from her hand. She had a tremendously strong grip on the knife, and I had to pry one bony finger at a time from the wooden handle.

As I got close to Ursula, she turned her head toward me and licked her cracked lips. She pressed her nose against my temple, took a slow deep breath, then whispered "Yum."

* * *

Life is a growing process. We all morph and change as we maneuver through our own existence. I'm not going to give up on this Violent One because I have faith in humanity. I have faith in Ursula.

* * *

SAN JUAN CAPISTRANO TRIBUNE

October 31, 2018

By Ebenezer Thompson

A 37 year old man identified as Jim Stevens was found dead in his apartment on Thursday afternoon, after the neighbors reported a foul smell emanating from his unit. Mr. Stevens's head had been decapitated and placed upon his dining room table.

The police are searching for a "Violent One," which is apparently an exotic pet from the Brazilian Rainforest, recently purchased by Mr. Stevens. The Violent One's name is Ursula. She was last seen running wildly from Mr. Stevens's apartment wielding a bloody knife. Ursula stands approximately 4 feet tall, with straight, bright green hair. She was last seen wearing a DIO concert T-shirt and green camouflage pants.

Anyone with information regarding the whereabouts of Ursula, or any other information regarding Mr. Stevens's death, is asked to please contact investigator Sherman Patterson at (555) 555–7503.

Lunch at the Vatican

HONEYMOONS OFTEN don't turn out so fantastic because they involve two unsuspecting young adults who have been through a lifetime of change within just a few short, hectic days.

Alice and Troy had a decent relationship, but not a great one. Troy initially thought he was making a great decision to spend the rest of his life with Alice, but he had some second thoughts after the proposal because Alice's epic blow jobs became a distant memory once the engagement ring was tightly secured to her left third finger.

Alice's grandparents were nice enough to spring for a 15 day honeymoon in Italy. Alice's grandfather ("Grandpa Ralph") bankrolled the honeymoon because he was proudly 100% Italian and 110% Catholic. Grandpa Ralph often bragged to the rest of the world that all non-Italians were inferior. And he despised Troy because he was Irish. Grandpa Ralph once went out of his way to ask Alice within earshot of Troy "Why are you marrying this Irish Mick?"

Troy overheard the remark but didn't care much because old Grandpa Ralph would be dead soon. Troy looked forward to secretly snickering to himself while standing before Grandpa Ralph's corpse at the funeral. There would be a secret middle finger salute shot at Grandpa Ralph, from Troy's hand hidden in his coat pocket.

* * *

Once in Italy, Troy could not help but notice that Rome was a dump. Beggars and gypsies everywhere, dirty streets, filthy cars, kitschy souvenir stands, crazy drivers and putrid sweaty heat.

"I want to see Vatican City today," said Alice on their first day in Rome.

"Can't we just see some of the ruins and take it easy," replied Troy.

"No, I want to see Vatican City today, in case we want to see it a second time before we catch the train to Florence."

"Okay, whatever," said Troy, realizing that this unpleasant encounter would be played on a continuous loop in varying versions until his death.

* * *

Troy and Alice were walking carelessly down a narrow street, following their map. They were supposedly right next to the Vatican, but they couldn't see it due to the surrounding buildings. A tall, thin man with dark skin and dark hair walked by them, wearing a black priest uniform. He looked so much like Father Damien from The Exorcist that Troy chuckled out loud to himself a little bit.

Alice asked "Excuse me, Father, which way toward the Vatican?"

The man stoically stood at attention and replied in broken English "walk two blocks down, turn right, then you see our beautiful Vatican City."

"Thank you, Father," Alice replied, bowing her head with reverence.

"What's with all the 'Father' this, and 'Father' that B.S.? You haven't been to church in 15 years," said Troy.

"Stop being such a flaming asshole. I know that's a tall order for you, so just do your best."

They continued walking down the narrow street as directed, when Troy realized that he was not only miserable, but hungry too. He spied a man wearing a white chef's uniform. Actually, it looked more like a costume, with a puffy white hat obnoxiously perched on top of his head, like Chef Boyardee. The man stood in front of a door with no sign, gesturing with both arms for Alice and Troy to enter. Troy walked past the man at a brisk pace, peeked his head inside the door, and saw rows of tables with people sitting and eating what looked like tasty food.

"I'm starving, let's grab a quick lunch before seeing

Liberace Palace," joked Troy.

"Your assholiness is on full display today," replied Alice.

The café was serving food cafeteria style. Troy eagerly grabbed a tray and started mowing his way through the salad section. There was no menu displayed on the wall and no prices listed. The café workers were lined up with plastic spoons and tongs in their hands, with guilty grins hidden just beneath their lips.

Before Alice made her way to the croutons, Troy had found a seat and was shoveling peas and pizza slices into his face at a rapid pace. Alice scooted slowly along the cafeteria line, with the friendly café workers offering pastries, slices of cake, pizza, pasta, and salad selections. She took a bit of everything.

"Right this way, Madame," said the man in the Chef Boyardee costume, as he directed Alice to the table where Troy was rapidly chewing and swallowing with great joy.

"Thanks for waiting for me, jerk," said Alice.

"Oh for the love of Jehovah, you're not six years old," said Troy, as a soggy clump of pizza tumbled from his face.

Alice started with her salad, which she had to admit was not bad. A slim man with a black shirt and dark, slicked back hair, approached their table. The man casually slid a piece of paper onto the table and said "when you are ready sir, you can pay at the front." He motioned toward the man in the Chef Boyardee costume. The man in the black shirt then gracefully floated away.

Troy picked up the piece of paper and stared at it in confused silence.

"What the hell is this? 127 Euros! 17 Euros for peas! 46 Euros for two slices of pizza!"

"Troy calm down, I'm sure there is some explanation. We can work something out with them," said Alice.

Troy looked around and noticed that other patrons of the café also had stunned looks on their faces, with their eyes bulging as they reviewed their checks.

The man in the black shirt noticed Troy yelling at the table, and walked over.

"Is there a problem, sir."

"Well, let's see. You are charging futuristic prices for your food. Apparently, someone told you it was the year 2253," replied Troy, as Alice's face became bright red.

"Sir, these are our prices and you must pay. If you had asked, we would have gladly provided you with the prices before you make purchase."

Troy sat there for a moment, trying to calm himself down. His brain felt like it was going to explode out of his skull and he could feel his face turning hot. Troy tried counting backwards from 10, like a psychologist had taught him to do when he would lose his temper in high school. That didn't work, either. Troy thought about being called a Mick by Grandpa Ralph, and about all of Alice's smartass remarks since the plane touched down in Italy.

Before he knew what was happening, Troy grabbed a plate full of Caesar salad and smashed it right into the face of the man wearing the black shirt. Big chunks of Caesar salad flew everywhere, like an exploding green volcano. Troy was surprised at how frozen the man stood in his place, as the whitish salad violently collided with his face. Like a mannequin, seemingly stunned by his own existence, with chunks of slimy salad stuck to his slick hair.

"ARRIVEDERCI, PRICK!" yelled Troy.

Chef Boyardee started to make his way toward the commotion when Troy swiped a plastic tray and whacked the top of his head. Troy felt like he was Hulk Hogan slamming the Iron Sheikh with a folding chair. He was surprised at how easily the top of the goofy white hat deflated.

"Don't just stand there, run!" Troy yelled at Alice.

The two of them burst out the front door of the café, onto the old Italian streets. Alice ran at full sprint for a good five minutes. Troy began gasping for breath after about 60 seconds. All those Sunday morning doughnuts.

"What the bloody fucking hell was that?" demanded Alice.

"I'm sorry babe, but those dirty crooks had it coming. Let's go back to the hotel room and I'll make it up to you. Me love you long time," said Troy grinning, while hunched over with his hands on his knees.

"My God, I've married a great big stupid man-child."

Troy stood upright and took a good look at Alice's gorgeous

white face covered with sexy freckles. She really did have the most beautiful blue eyes. Troy placed both hands on her firm ass, squeezed gently, and kissed her mouth.

"I'm all yours baby, I'm all yours," said Troy.

There and Back

I AM GOING to tell you about something that happened last year. Most folks would not believe a story like this, but most folks also don't understand that it just might be the sun that revolves around the earth, after all.

* * *

I was starting to feel better as I drove to Pete's house. There was something soothing about driving alone at night in the cold. When you get older, privacy becomes a rare and precious commodity.

Pete's desperate eyes peered through the curtains and out his living room window. Before I had finished pulling up to the curb, Pete slithered through the front door and down his porch steps before his wife could notice he was gone.

"Iron Maiden, dude, this is going to be epic," said Pete.

We were off to Irvine Meadows Amphitheater to see our childhood Metal heroes who had become 60-year-old men with thinning hair, wearing tight pants and T-shirts with no sleeves.

"Fifth row! Man, we are going to be right there," said Pete. "I'll be stoked if Steve Harris points his bass right at me when he scans the crowd."

"How's work," I asked.

"To quote the great Huey Lewis and the News—I'm takin' what their givin' cause I'm workin' for a livin'," answered Pete. "How have you been, bro?"

"My back and neck hurt me all the time, if only I could trade in this shitty body for a new one," I said.

Pete contemplated this, then added "Think of it this way— your body only has to
last you a few more decades, then you will get a nice long rest."

"Thanks, that makes me feel much better. At least I can still jam on my guitar," I said.

* * *

I used to play an old Fender Jazz Master guitar I had stumbled upon at a local pawn shop. It was chipped and ripped and rusted. Old and green, it was just like that down-trodden guitar Kurt Cobain played. Kurt always looked so happily angst-ridden with his greasy blond hair, post-pubescent beard stubble, and grandpa-garage sale green sweater vest. I put together a band and we practiced in the garage and played a few parties. We really thought we had made it big when our band's name was up in lights on the marquee of The Troubadour in L.A.

Predictably, age and reality stole our dreams of music

fame.

* * *

The Irvine Meadows parking lot was a bona fide time capsule. Metal music with demonic themes blasted from surrounding cars. Something looked different, though. Everyone was older, way older! We had become part of a mob of middle aged dads with eyeglasses, goaties and fat guts, wearing Iron Maiden T-shirts. Age transforms everyone in a cruel but unique way. People ultimately stop existing in their true form and become low-quality, broken versions of themselves.

We eventually made our way through the urine and beer smelling parking lot and passed the merchandise stands.

"$50 T-shirts! The whole world is nuts," I said.

"We can buy two beers for $50 instead," laughed Pete.

The beer was cold but sad. The secret behind alcohol's success is that every drink tells a lie to the drinker. A drink at a happening bar or nightclub deviously convinces the drinker that there is world full of amazing opportunities. However, beer sitting in a big and flimsy paper cup at an Iron Maiden concert does not even try to lie. It just says: *Dude, if you're drinking me, things have not worked out well for you.*

At least the tickets were good, fifth row in fact. Darkness— explosions—bright lights—loud noise—old dudes playing air drums. It was all there, just like I remembered it 25 years before. Pete's excited hand sloshed some beer onto his shoes. We slapped high-fives with unfamiliar concertgoers who shared our enthusiasm for outdated man-metal.

* * *

I drove Pete back to his house around 1 A.M. He was disappointed to return home and I could tell. I suggested that we go surfing early the following morning. We agreed to meet at Trestles at 5:30 AM.

"See you bright and early, bro."

* * *

Trestles is one of the best surf breaks in California. The wave has nice power with near perfect shape at multiple peaks.

I met Pete at the Trestles parking lot bright and early and we began our 1 mile foot journey down to the sand. This particular Saturday morning was damn crowded. The sand was cold but soothing on my bare feet. The sun was rising at our backs and there was no wind.

I was beginning to notice that full body wetsuits were becoming increasingly difficult to negotiate onto my joints as I got older. Still, I managed to squeeze into mine after a struggle. I was still skinny, but Pete had become rather lumpy. He would say that he had become "barrel chested." Pete had purchased an XXL wetsuit to accommodate his growing torso, and he eventually slithered himself into the thing.

Nietzsche once said that a man's belly is the only thing preventing him from thinking that he is God, and Nietzsche was right.

The initial shock of the freezing cold Pacific Ocean still makes my head scream after all these years. We made our way past the whitewash, just out to where the waves were breaking. The waves were decent size, but not huge. The water was smooth and reflective.

I saw a real nice one coming my way and I paddled hard for it. The force of the water thrust me upward and outward, toward the shore. The ride was smooth and peaceful. All sound stopped and my vision became hyper focused on the half-tube of liquid glass.

When the wave died out, I paddled back to Pete. "That was a nice one, man. I hope that it gets bigger as the tide comes in," said Pete.

Pete and I sat on our boards, quietly bobbing up and down in the water for what seemed like a long time. We were surrounded by about 15 other surfers at the same break, but they were all just chilling too.

A surf line up is one of the last places where communication technology has no place. If someone paddled out on a surfboard talking on a waterproof phone I really do think that person would get his ass kicked.

We sat and waited and waited and waited. We stared at the ocean, but the ocean was cold and did not stare back.

Finally, a slick, dark blue mountain slowly began forming in the distance. Pete and I quickly lied down and our boards. We paddled fast and hard toward the approaching force. This wave was going to be a big one and both of us knew it. In fact, this wave was abnormally large, considering the modest waves generated by that day's swell.

Pete and I were paddling almost 15 feet apart, heading straight toward the peak of the wave. This wave was too big and was breaking too far out. It was going to break before we could reach it and suck us into the whitewash and pummel us around a bit.

But the wave did not start to break as expected. It kept lurching forward and growing mightier. Pete saw that I was turning around to try to catch it and gave me a look that said *are you crazy?* Well, Pete must have been crazy too, because he flipped his board around and paddled frantically toward the shore.

The peak of the wave split me and Pete in two directions— Pete went left and I went right. The front part of my feet and especially my toes kept me from losing my balance. I barely hung on but managed to have a good ride.

I paddled back to the point slowly. Pete caught up and met me there. "That thing was huge," Pete exclaimed.

"It started to close out and I couldn't make the next section so I bailed out early," I added.

As we both sat staring into the horizon looking for the next wave, Pete asked "where did everybody go?"

"That wave must have taken us down to the next peak away from the crowd," I said.

"I don't think so. This is the same point that we took off from, and there are no surfers, anywhere," said Pete.

"Oh well, more waves for us."

A few more good ones came our way and my old creaky joints got a good workout that morning. I finally let a small wave scoot me toward shore. I had to stop half way because the tide was still low enough to expose about 20 yards of barnacle-covered boulders. I was able to maneuver over them easily with thick rubber booties protecting my feet.

As I sat on the sand and waited for Pete to get out of the water, I realized that Pete had been right. There was no one else in the water. Or on the beach. Not a single soul. Pete made his way to shore and began walking up the hill of sand, toward the spot where our towels and clothes had been left.

"Did someone steal our stuff?" Pete asked.

I wasn't sure what was happening, but I felt completely out of sorts and everything looked familiar and unfamiliar at the same time.

As Pete and I walked along the sand toward the trail to the parking lot, we couldn't find the trail. It was just trees and bushes. The houses on the bluffs were gone. The power lines and train tracks had vanished, too.

"Did the current take us south into Camp Pendleton Marine Base?" asked Pete.

"This is the same spot, I am sure of it," I said.

But I wasn't sure of anything at that moment. The beach was naked and the sky looked like it had been waiting for us.

We walked up the sand mound to the level ground. The sun was blindingly bright. We were alone. The railroad trestle was gone, or more accurately, had never been there.

We pressed forward, nervously peeling off our wetsuits. Mine clung to my sore, wet body like plastic wrap. Pete and I kept our wetsuits on at the waist, since our clothes had vanished.

We walked, then sat, and then waited, for nothing in particular. Pete and I sat and said nothing, both of us knowing that something was terribly wrong.

Thirst suddenly hit both of us fast and hard. It had been hot and sunny out in the water, and neither of us had anything but coffee to drink before paddling out. The sharp claws of the putrid thirst plunged deep into my throat and mouth. Unlike the feeling of hunger, the sensation of thirst lets you know that you will die soon without water.

I saw some weird-looking maroon colored fruit hanging from a short tree. I stood up, picked one off, and took a bite. It tasted like rotten mango, and I tossed one to Pete. He gobbled up the fruit like a hungry basset hound attacking corned beef dropped onto the kitchen floor.

After sitting for a few more minutes, Pete asked: "What are you thinking?" *My head is a bad neighborhood and you don't want to know.* But I had actually stopped thinking a few minutes before. We both got up and walked over a small sand dune and into the weeds.

Our surfboards were left behind, looking abandoned and lonely on the white sand.

Through the brush Pete spotted something that was brown and rounded out. The Thing was a massive mound of long, reddish brown fur, about 8 feet tall and 3 feet wide.

It was hunched over some sort of machine with two screens. Pete looked back at me with his index finger placed over his lips. *SHHH!*

The Thing looked as if he were fiddling and tinkering with a bunch of metal instruments. Patiently watching the screens for any sign of whatever he was looking for. It was motionless, like a hairy caveman in a museum nature scene. Innocent and dumb, but potentially dangerous too.

The Thing was alone, but there were signs of other hairy kin nearby—a few straw beds, food and tools scattered about.

There was a forceful smell of some strange sort of fleshy BBQ, and I spied thick grey smoke rising from behind a stack of boulders.

We approached The Thing slowly from the side and the images on the screens came into focus. One screen showed surfers bobbing up and down in the water at Trestles, where we were a lifetime ago. The second screen showed the same beach, but empty. Peering around the boulders, I spotted a second furry creature cantilevering his face directly over the thick BBQ smoke and lusting after the large chunks of broiling meat.

I took two steps closer, but my feet made too much noise so I stopped. I looked toward Pete, and he was frozen in time like a sloppily made wax figure, where the cheeks and eyes just don't look quite human.

My head slowly turned back toward the furry mound. Before I could focus my eyes, I noticed something very strong. That smell! Possibly the most horrific nasal sensation of all time. A combination of feces and death mixed with rotten heat.

Suddenly I was confronted with two big, dark brown watery eyes within a foot of my forehead. Under the eyes sat a mouth that formed a child's happy grin.

I felt as if I were in one of those dreams where I frantically try to run but my legs won't cooperate. In those dreams, I eventually start to run on my hands. But this was no dream, and I was paralyzed from head to toe with pure dread.

There would be no magical hand-running in this nightmare. Just pain, screaming, and agony while floating aimlessly through some time-wedge in a distant universe.

Pete's feet stayed cemented to the wet dirt. What Pete must have noticed first was how the size of the encroaching mass blocked all sunlight from his face. The Thing slowly crept forward, with one hand fumbling for something behind his back. Pete wondered what it could be. A weapon? Poison?

The Thing seemed to have no consideration for the misery we were about to endure, just a curiosity as to who would be the tastiest. I swore I could see random thoughts bouncing slowly behind the Thing's placid eyes—*the one on the left is sure portly.*

There was a tingling sensation at my legs that shot down into each individual toe. It was a sensation I had during dreams about slipping off the side of a high-rise building, or off a bridge. A feeling of terror and impending free fall, with the sense that my stomach was floating helplessly up to the infinite.

I tried to scream, but all I could do was shout a series of completely unintelligible sounds out of my face. I must have been half screaming and half crying a parade of mad sound bites. The horrific smell surrounded me good and tight. I felt the fur brush up against me and I knew my demise would come soon.

EEEKKKKKKKHH!! The Thing then let out a horrid shriek. I had quickly grabbed a jagged piece of bamboo and thrust it through the webbing of The Thing's toes. It wasn't blood that came out, but a purple gel, which blended with the brown fur, creating a blackish substance.

The Thing suddenly forgot all about us, and grabbed his foot and howled. It hopped up and down on the other foot before falling onto its butt to inspect the wound.

"Run to the water, go, now!" I ordered Pete.

But Pete was already gone, running faster than I had ever seen him. Small spoonfuls of white sand flickered from beneath Pete's feet—arms like angry snakes thrusting back and forth, sweeping his torso.

A rough strip of flesh swiped my calf. The Thing's hand had hit me hot like a burning fire poker. My stomach and chin were dragging across the sand now. The sand was smooth except for the jagged branches and bamboo that were cutting my abdomen.

There was a short piece of time that I cannot remember. I had wiggled or fought my way free somehow, because what I do remember is flying and screaming across the sand toward the water, with my legs racing under me. I passed Pete. The glistening water was almost within reach now.

The Thing may have been chasing us, but I didn't look back to see. The water splashed my face and Pete was swimming beside me. I finally looked back and saw an empty beach. Well, not completely empty.

The Thing stood at the shore, peering at us with confused eyes, the cold water nipping at his furry toes. He still had that childish grin on his face, and I could almost envision him holding a bunch of yellow balloons and waving bye-bye to us.

The sun was bright and my eyes were burning real bad. The water was flat like a lake. Pete and I bobbed up and down in the water without saying a word. Then, a blue water mountain slowly rose on the horizon, but we no longer had our surfboards.

"Hey Pete, do you remember body surfing at The Wedge in Newport?"

"Shit yea!" Pete replied.

We swam directly toward shore kicking our feet like a couple of old white potato mashers, letting the cold blue water race by us. This wave was bigger than the last one, and picked us up and shot us forward. I put out my left hand and curved that way, and Pete went right. We kept flying down, down, down that water mountain.

Then BOOM! That wave crashed hard, flinging us through the whitewash, back and forth and up and down. I actually punched myself in the forehead, just above my right eye. At one point, my back was pinned right up against the rocks. I tried to reach the surface, but the more I swam, the more water there was. I started to crave oxygen as if I would explode without it, but I just kept swimming with both cheeks puffed out.

Finally, my left hand peaked through the top of the water, then my right hand, and my head followed. That smoggy Southern California air never tasted so good. I stumbled onto shore and just sat there.

Pete was about 50 feet south, marching his way out of the whitewash. He saw me and waved, with a big stupid look on his face.

All the other surfers were back in the water now, the hot babes in bikinis were back on the sand, and the lifeguard was sitting on his stand catching some rays. The Thing was nowhere in sight.

My cheeks got tight, my chin trembled, and I started weeping like a baby.

Pete sat next to me for a long while in silence, then said "Hey Cameron, let's go get some fish tacos and drink some Coronas."

"You read my mind, bro."

The Patient One

"WHY ISN'T my baby crying? He's just grunting," screamed Darla.

The midwife whisked little Timothy to a table in the delivery room for a closer examination.

"He was stuck in the birth canal for quite awhile. The doctor will be right in to examine him," replied the midwife.

Timothy's breath became increasingly slow and casual. The Patient One made his way from the corner of the room, inching closer to Timothy. The Patient One descended upon Timothy swiftly, bringing overbearing darkness to the small room.

Suddenly, Timothy's breathing strengthened and his eyes opened curiously. The tired, new mother smothered her new, strong baby with tearful cuddles and kisses. The Patient One returned to his corner and sat quietly.

* * *

Timothy got his first car at the age of sixteen, but driving was just too boring. He couldn't resist the temptation of motorcycles. One cold Sunday morning, Timothy was racing through Ortega Canyon Highway on his Japanese "crotch rocket." There was barely sufficient sunlight for him to see where he was going.

The Patient One glided from mountain to mountain, hovering low and watching Timothy.

The motorcycle's rear tire slid over dry dirt and loose rocks and started to fishtail. Timothy was flung to the asphalt like a rag doll. He rolled and tumbled, snapping bones and tearing skin.

Timothy lied there, sprawled out on the lonely highway, in front of a blind corner. Around the bend, a moving van approached at a steady clip.

The Patient One descended from the nearest hill with wings spread wide. The Patient One landed gently on the asphalt, taking purposeful steps toward Timothy's limp body. The van whipped itself around the sharp turn. The driver spied Timothy, quickly slammed the brakes, and stopped with just a few feet to spare.

The Patient One stepped back, then returned to the top of the mountain and watched. Timothy was damn lucky.

* * *

Decades passed slowly, like floats in a parade. Timothy dutifully manoeuvred through each phase of life. He walked his daughter down the aisle. Climbed Mt. McKinley. Endured chemo and radiation therapy for testicular cancer. Lost his job.

Battled alcoholism. Stood second row at the Stones concert and saw Mick and Keith up close and personal one last time before they faded into history forever.

The Patient One was always there. Watching. Waiting for the designated moment.

Somehow Timothy woke up one morning and he was seventy, with high cholesterol and sciatica. Timothy's wife insisted on a gym membership, and she could be a formidable foe. So Timothy did what he was told and frequented the gym three days a week.

At 5:45 AM on Sunday morning, Timothy had the indoor pool all to himself. After a brief warm up, he swam hard. Ten minutes later, he felt a pulled a muscle in his chest. Then tightness and pain along the left arm. The copper-like smell that followed was overbearing and confusing.

Lying face down in the pool, Timothy was drowsy and unable to move.

It was time.

The Patient One nudged through the wall like a ghost, surveying the blue water. Timothy floated lifelessly. Arms dangling, head sunk. The Patient One entered the water and caressed Timothy, embracing him with large black wings. Timothy vaguely sensed a heavy, sinking feeling.

He was too weak and too tired to fight The Patient One this time.

The Patient One looked upward with glassy black eyes

darker than infinity, grasped Timothy tightly, and flew with the speed of the universe into the cosmos.

Frankie and the Bass

THAT MUST BE A BASS because it has four fat strings, thought Frankie.

The bass was clunky and ugly, sitting in the window at The Music House on Lake Forest Blvd. The old junker was black and white. Actually not even white, but some depressing mixture of beige and buttermilk. The edges were softly rounded like the back of the new AMC Pacer parked in Frankie's neighbor's driveway. It was the kind of bass that Mr. Rodgers would softly strum with his thumb while whisper-singing like half a man.

No flames, no neon finish, no sharp, pointy edges. Frankie's MTV heavy metal heroes would definitely not be drowning in an avalanche of hot babes if they were forced to play such dull looking hunks of timber.

But the price was probably right.

Frankie knew he could never save the $345 he would need to get his hands on that red Fender Precision Bass he had seen at "Hoc It To Doc" pawn shop last month.

Frankie moseyed into The Music House to get a closer peek. The store smelled like old records and dirty carpet. Wall-to-wall guitars, basses and amps. A few drum sets in the back. Music books, instructional tapes and videos, kazoos, jew's harps, harmonicas, tuners, and strings.

Behind the counter stood an old dude. But then again, everyone over 25 looked like a fossilized relic to Frankie. But this guy actually *was* pretty damn old, with long, thin light brown hair revealing generous chunks of pale scalp. The Fu Manchu mustache did not exactly make him look like a spring chicken, either.

Fu Manchu Dude wore tight brown corduroy pants and a floral long sleeved shirt. The type of shirt that Robert Plant would wear while femininely dancing around on stage while John Bonham bashed away on the drums like a caveman. The leather vest with an enormous peace sign back patch was a nice touch, too. And don't forget the cowhide moccasins to complete the 1969 casualty-of-the-Woodstock-generation costume.

"Jimmy Page was the best of all-time, period," Fu Manchu Dude said to a teenage kid casually strumming a Gibson flying V.

"No way, man. Have you heard Joe Satriani," said the kid.

"That Satriani clown can play all the notes he wants at lightning speed. Page would blow him out of the water any day with style! Your generation is getting ripped off with some seriously crappy music," said Fu Manchu Dude.

"Page was pretty good in his day, but you've gotta get with the times, man! 'Satch' is the future of guitar," said the teenage kid.

"Pretty good in his day? Put that guitar back on the rack and scram," said Fu Manchu Dude.

"Don't take it personally, bro, it's just my opinion," said the teenage kid, grabbing his backpack and walking out the door.

"Can I help you, man?" asked Fu Manchu Dude, turning to Frankie.

"Is that black and white guitar in the window a bass?" asked Frankie.

"Yup. Four strings means it's a bass, bro. Do you know how to count to four? Come back with your parents and maybe I'll cut them a deal. Moms like me," said Fu Manchu Dude.

Frankie fumbled with his sweaty hands in the pockets of his Levi's jacket, feeling very unimportant. Fu Manchu dude wandered crookedly into the back of the shop, where Frankie could hear rummaging.

The store had quickly become empty. The bass sat in the window by the front door, seeming lonely. Frankie had grown mighty tired of taking it on the chin from the Fu Manchu Dudes of the world.

Frankie's feet stepped with urgency toward the window and his hands removed themselves from the pockets of his Levi's jacket. His armpits felt swampy and his heart kicked enthusiastically against his sternum. Frankie reached out and gently lifted the bass by the neck, caressing it with both hands. The bass felt warm and grateful. Frankie's legs took him quickly out the front door and onto the sidewalk.

Frankie glanced through the glass door and saw Fu Manchu Dude's beady little blue eyes beaming at him. Fu Manchu Dude started running toward the door.

"Don't even think about it, twerp," yelled Fu Manchu Dude.

The truth was, Frankie had not really give much thought to what he was doing. His feet carried him like a racing greyhound across the empty sidewalk. A cold and dry winter wind stung Frankie's soft, delicate face.

A quick glance back, and Frankie saw Fu Manchu Dude not really running, but instead having a series of controlled falls using his helplessly skinny legs for support. Long, wispy hair sadly waving in the cool breeze like a white middle-aged flag of surrender.

Fu Manchu Dude then started wheezing, as his lungs turned to fire. He could then only walk at a brisk pace. All those clove cigarettes.

Frankie coolly glided onto the sidewalk beside Lake Forest Blvd., as a public bus slowly came to a stop in front of Del Taco. Frankie hopped onto the bus and tossed three quarters into the payment funnel next to the driver's stick shift.

Fu Manchu Dude watched Frankie trot up the steps and onto the bus. Fu Manchu Dude heaved on the sidewalk with spit dangling from his mouth, bent over with his hands gripping his corduroy covered knees.

Frankie caressed the stolen bass in his arms and studied its

THEY ARE HERE NOW

cracked finish with a lover's gaze. It was meant to be his. The bass promised a future of late night rehearsals, gigs, and of course, girls. Lots of hysterical, cheering girls.

The Indestructible Frankie Lixx

FRANKIE LIXX LOATHED meetings with the record company executives. The uppity board room. The rows of man-drones wearing three piece suits and sporting Steve McQueen haircuts. The hum of the A/C blowing stale air beneath soul crushing florescent lights. As a thrice platinum rock star, Frankie Lixx expected five things out of life: money, drugs, vodka, party girls, and fast cars.

Wilshire Boulevard was a nightmare at 10 AM. *DO PEOPLE REALLY WAKE UP THIS EARLY EVERY DAY TO GO TO WORK?* Frankie Lixx zoomed his gleaming white Pantera with shiny chrome wheels up to the valet booth. A Mondale/Ferraro '84 bumper sticker adorned the rear bumper.

"Mr. Lixx, it's great to see you again. My kids love your new album. Hey, man, what happened to your arm?," asked the valet.

"Just a little boo-boo, dude," replied Frankie Lixx with a cocaine grin, tossing the keys to the valet.

* * *

Stan was there to greet Frankie Lixx as the elevator doors parted ways on the 23rd floor.

"Frankie baby! How's that arm doing? I thought we had

agreed to meet at 9 AM. Anyway, don't worry about it. The boys are ready for us in the boardroom."

Frankie Lixx entered the boardroom and greeted everyone by waiving with a limp and uncommitted left hand.

All the men took their seats, and a bald man with a perfectly round torso stood at the head of a comically long boardroom table.

"I'll get started. Frankie, I was sorry to hear about your motorcycle crash last weekend on the Sunset strip. Look, if you guys want to get high and drink and bang strippers all over L.A., be my guest. Just don't do it while cruising on a chopper! This record company has invested more money in your band than Dolly Parton spends on bras, which makes you OUR asset," said the bald, round man.

Frankie Lixx just sat there, slumped in a big red tufted leather chair, high from the pain pills his doctor had prescribed. He had gulped down half the bottle of pills in one night. Frankie's dark sunglasses covered his bloodshot eyes, which had closed and transformed into a pair of dark slits.

"The tour kicks off in two weeks, and we can't cancel the dates. The concert crew is run by the Teamsters, and the Teamsters answer to those Italian fellows who drive Cadillacs and carry chrome plated pistols, if you catch my drift. We owe a ton of dough in advance for these dates, come rain or shine, broken arm or not. So we cannot and will not cancel any of the shows," said the bald, round man.

Frankie Lixx snapped out of his trance and stood bolt upright, forcing the leather chair to shoot backward and crash to the floor.

"I hate dealing with you suits. Do any of you guys actually play an instrument, or do you just drive around in your station wagons all day, whistling along to Kenny Rogers? I built The Durty Bastards from nothing in my parents' garage, and I won't stand by and watch some hired gun hack fill in for me on bass!"

"Sit down, Frankie, and listen closely. As far as the fans will know, Frankie Lixx will be playing bass at each and every scheduled show, from Boise to Tulsa. We found a guy who looks just like you, only he is a little bit shorter. With the right wig, makeup, big dark sunglasses and stage costumes, your drunken fans will never know the difference. Don't worry about his playing ability, either. We'll have your bass tracks pre-programmed, so all this dunce needs to do is dance around a little bit, make kissy faces at the broads in the front row, and try to look like you while he's holding the bass," said the bald, round man.

"You mean all this two bit impostor needs to do is hold MY BASS, the one that spells FRANKIE LIXX on the motherfucking fretboard, and do his best to bamboozle my audience! If word ever gets out about this, The Durty Bastards will be finished!" screamed Frankie.

"Relax. We've already had a little pow wow with the fellas at Metal Masters Magazine, and they know everything. They have agreed to keep their collective traps shut. In exchange, The Durty Bastards will grant them multiple exclusive interviews with each member of the band, and exclusive photo shoots when the new album is released. Aside from the few heavy metal reporters out there, no one else will be investigating this. Hell Frankie, it's not like Woodward and Bernstein are going to burn much shoe leather getting to the bottom of this mystery. Frankie, this is a done deal. Get yourself down to the Bahamas, get some sun, meet some babes, and drink some Mai Tais on the beach. Come back to L.A. in three months tanned, rested, healed, and ready to rejoin The Durty Bastards on the second leg of the tour."

Frankie Lixx scanned the boardroom, studying the faces of six sweaty men wearing cheap polyester suits, before making an undramatic exit. He stepped into the elevator, retrieved his Pantera from the valet, then slowly drove down Wilshire Boulevard toward his empty mansion in Bel Air. Frankie Lixx slept soundly until 8 PM, waking up just in time to catch a new episode of Airwolf on T.V.

* * *

There was no trip to the Bahamas for Frankie Lixx. No Mai Tais on the beach, and no rest and relaxation. Frankie Lixx spent the next several weeks sitting and brooding in his Bel Air mansion, trying to devise a plan to prevent a low life doppelgänger from stealing his identity as the bass player for The Durty Bastards.

One night while watching a ninja movie marathon, Frankie Lixx was struck with a fantastic idea. The next day, he made his way to the library and conducted some research regarding Japanese poison ninja darts. After some tinkering with a narrow PVC pipe, sewing needles, and a concoction of rat poison, Frankie Lixx's plan was almost complete.

The Durty Bastards had a gig at the L.A. Forum on New Year's Eve. Frankie Lixx used his band ID to enter through the loading zone. He wore a black L.A. Kings hat with a long black trench coat. The kid watching the back door wasn't paying attention, and Frankie Lixx walked right on by. He stood at stage left with his hat pulled down low over his brow, and his face glaring at the floor.

The lights dimmed and the crowd roared with anticipation. Thousands of Bic lighters created a constellation of yellow stars splattering a black ocean of anonymous concertgoers. The Durty Bastards took the stage with the "fake" Frankie Lixx on bass. Frankie Lixx stood about 10 feet away from his impostor, as the band opened with the first song on the setlist, KNEEL DOWN PUSSYCAT.

The fake Frankie Lixx had an enormous, sinister grin plastered across his face and his eyes were bugging out of his head like an overly caffeinated Gene Wilder. He was grinding his pelvis into the back of Frankie Lixx's bass, while pointing at the cute girls in the front row and motioning with his index finger. *YES, I WANT YOU!*

Frankie Lixx felt his entire body become hot and sweaty with rage. *THAT TWO BIT HUSTLER IS TRYING TO STEAL MY LIFE, BUT NOW IT'S PAYBACK TIME.*

Frankie Lixx slowly and deliberately inched his left hand into the inside pocket of his black trench coat, removing a plastic baggie containing three needles that had been dipped in rat poison and cyanide. With his left hand, he produced a narrow, 18 inch long PVC pipe from a strap inside his trench coat. Frankie Lixx's hands started to tremble and his breathing became labored. *I ONLY HAVE THREE CHANCES TO GET THIS RIGHT. TAKE A DEEP BREATH AND AIM FOR THE NECK.*

A massive cloud of air filled Frankie Lixx's diaphragm and lungs. He placed one end of the PVC pipe to his lips, where he created a tight and deliberate seal. Frankie Lixx closed one eye and did the best he could to aim the tip of the pipe toward the neck of the fake Frankie Lixx. A massive pocket of air exploded into Frankie Lixx's mouth, then to his lips, then straight through the PVC pipe. Frankie Lixx quickly placed the pipe back into the strap inside his trench coat before anyone could see. *I THINK I MISSED. I HAVE JUST TWO MORE CHANCES.*

Before Frankie Lixx had a chance to reload his pipe with a new poison needle, the fake Frankie Lixx suddenly fell to his knees and unstrapped the bass from around his neck. He then collapsed face down onto the stage, with the stage lights painting the top of his head with a penumbra of obnoxious rainbow colors. His arms and legs shook uncontrollably, with his face staring straight into the dirty black stage, like a child

looking for his pet frog through the top of a fishbowl.
Paramedics rushed onto the stage.

The fake Frankie Lixx left the lighted stage one last time, on a stretcher.

The rest of the band just stood there, stunned. Frankie Lixx removed the black trench coat that had been hiding his stage clothes — a black and blue leather ensemble splattered with metal studs and spikes, with platform boots in the shape of a dragon's head with long, sharp teeth. Frankie Lixx threw his dark black sunglasses onto the bridge of his nose and teased his hair with a comb he whipped out from his back pocket. He had removed his arm cast the previous night with a hacksaw.

Walking onto the stage, Frankie Lixx noticed the shocked looks on the faces of his bandmates. The concertgoers in the first few rows looked equally flabbergasted. Frankie Lixx coolly picked up his bass and placed the leather strap over his left shoulder. His platform boots were placed two feet apart, creating an obnoxiously wide stance. The bass was hung low, settling between his knees. At 6 foot 3 inches, Frankie Lixx looked like the most badass bass player in the history of Rock. He approached the front of the stage and placed his right hand over the mic.

"I AM THE ORIGINAL, INDESTRUCTIBLE FRANKIE LIXX, AND WE ARE THE DURTY BASTARDS. ONE, TWO, THREE, FOUR..."

The Durty Bastards tore straight into a Rock anthem that

can only be described as pure Americana, STRIPPING ON SUNSET. Young men in the front row slapped high fives and drank ice cold Coors Light from disintegrating paper cups, while young women shrieked hysterically and flashed their bras at the band.

Frankie Lixx and The Durty Bastards where back.

Floating In a Blue Dream

THE LIFE OF A WORKING MUSICIAN is nothing to be revered. Forget what you see on the Grammys. There are no after parties, no gift bags, no cheering fans, and certainly no awards. Just week after soul crushing week of giving $40 guitar lessons to spoiled tweens who spend most of the designated hour staring at their phones. And endless nights in bar band purgatory jamming "Play That Funky Music White Boy" until last call at 2 A.M. Then chasing down the deadbeat bar manager to get the band's $200 for the night.

Dale found himself pushing through another Wednesday night, standing on a dirty black stage beneath dull red and blue lights at The Beatnik Bar in Laguna Beach. He was playing rhythm guitar with Joe Steel and the Bandits, wrapping up a fourth and final set with The Stones's "Honky Tonk Woman." Strumming that song was a real hassle because it forced Dale to re-tune his Telecaster to the open G tuning that was invented by some long forgotten dude but made famous by Keith Richards in the 70s.

When that last song limped its way toward a technical finish, there was no applause or cheering, just the clattering of a few glasses scooped up by a weary eyed waitress who was way too sexy to ever be sighted socially in such a dump.

These late nights were really hitting Dale hard now that he had earned a one way ticket on the Geezerville Express. Age is a foul mouthed old bitch hell bent on taking what is hers. As soon as Dale shut the front door to his apartment at 3 A.M., the ringing in his ears engulfed his head with a tremendous roar.

* * *

The harsh morning sun violated the peaceful bedroom, as Dale lied in bed refusing to acknowledge that he was already awake. So he just lingered under the sheets and endured all sorts of thoughts. The thoughts shot at him fast and erratic, without any real connection between them, like random flickering images splattering against a wall. Dale's head had become a non-stop loop of bad movie trailers. *What would have become of the United States if Jimmy Carter had defeated Ronald Reagan in 1980? Do those new Honda hydrogen cars explode when they crash? Why had it taken so long for scientists to discover the chicken pox vaccine?*

After another night of insomnia and unchecked angst, Dale's eyes felt bloodshot before they were even open. This would be a four cup of coffee kind of a day, with one of those 5-Hour Energy bullshit things around 3 PM.

The Mental Misery Outlet was open for business.

After polishing off a bowl of LIFE cereal and a plain bagel,

Dale pawed past some pill bottles to grab a joint from his medicine cabinet. Dale felt like his pot somehow had a more respectable and justified existence if he housed it in close quarters with more legitimate medicine. So there sat Dale's little bag of brown joints, next to bottles full of chemicals with labels like DayQuil and Robitussin.

* * *

Dale made his first trip to the new marijuana dispensary on the corner, across from the 7–11. He had expected a tattoo parlor type of ambiance, but was pleasantly surprised. Real hardwood floor—that expensive, dark "distressed" stuff made of boards that looked as if they had been pried from an ancient shipwreck. Fancy bright lights and spotless glass display counters. Two heavily armed guards with guns visible, wearing Kevlar ammo vests and great big smiles. "Good morning, Sir."

Behind the counter, She stood at attention, ready to greet Dale. She, with the radiant flowing black hair, slender milky arms, perfect rows of glistening white teeth, lush lips, bright blue sapphire eyes, and breasts that stood bolt upright at all times day and night, looking as if they had been expecting Dale at any moment.

She talked while Dale stuttered and grimaced with an occasional, random half smile. "This here is called 'Blue Dream.' It will make you nice and relaxed—you'll love it!" But

Dale wasn't thinking about pot anymore. The skin of Her neck was tight and firm like a snare drum and Dale just stared and wondered how she would feel under his calloused fingers. Dale bought whatever She had recommended without saying a word and sheepishly exited the dispensary.

* * *

Dale had planned to smoke an occasional joint on weekends, but the stuff was just too wonderful and it overtook him rapidly. It didn't take long until Dale surrendered to an eventual "wake and bake" routine. Dale rolled out of bed each morning and ceremoniously held the joint between his thumb and index finger. The soft rolling paper caressed Dale's skin and he could sense the gentle relief the Blue Dream joint was just waiting to release. The Zippo lighter flicked that all too familiar sound of hollow steel under Dale's thumb and the flame shot high and straight. The tip of the joint stood out of Dale's mouth like a stiff diving board. The steady flame seemed to magically find its way to the end of the joint instinctively.

Every dancer in this elegant ballet knew her place and executed her moves flawlessly. The soothing smoke from the Blue Dream joint tasted like a chocolate milkshake in heaven and smelled like a deserted Tahitian beach at midnight. Dale's body floated and his mind focused, and all physical and mental pain evaporated into the cosmos. Dale saw colors and floating orbs and psychedelic swirls. Crickets danced and frogs roared and a steady calmness settled into Dale's core.

The Mental Misery Outlet was closed until further notice.

Lloyd Knocks Twice

PAWING THROUGH the daily Orange County Register, Lloyd grasped the Real Estate section and read the obnoxious headline with a twisted scowl: *Median Price For O.C. Home $783,000.*

"Jesus H. Christ on a bicycle, the whole world has gone screwy. How in the hell is any young family supposed to afford that?" Lloyd muttered to himself.

Lloyd wondered why he even bothered reading the daily newspaper anymore. But then again, he knew why. If the whole damn country wanted to devolve into an illiterate bunch of smartphone zombies, Lloyd Z. Patterson would not be joining their ranks. Anyone with half a brain knew that newspapers were the only place left for finding real news.

Then again, if Lloyd were being honest with himself, he had been marinating his senior brain in quite a bit of cable news since his retirement from Boeing in September. Lloyd considered himself a bonafide expert in all things current— global warming, droughts, nukes in North Korea, pollution, corruption in congress, the skyrocketing cost of living, and prescription drugs killing everyone and their mother. Lloyd missed the good old days and he didn't see the point in trying to hide it.

Lloyd met the love of his life, Connie, fresh out of high school in 1966. Connie had class. She always wore a new, crisp dress and high heels, with perfect makeup. Not a single hair out of place. Connie was beautiful, but she had always been modest about her looks. She was a dish.

Lloyd's father had secured him a lower level management job at Boeing at the tender age of 19. He and Connie married and bought themselves a nice house in Rossmoor, just three miles from the beach. Lloyd and Connie raised their two kids in that home without much fuss. America had just finished showing the whole wide world who was in charge and was kicking serious ass. Lloyd sure missed those days. Breast cancer finally caught up with Connie a few years back and transformed her into a tortured skeleton before finishing her off for good.

Since Connie's passing, Lloyd would rise from his lonesome bed around 9 o'clock and enter his bathroom to be greeted by a tidy caravan of orange pill bottles. A pill for blood pressure, a pill for cholesterol. Another one for arthritis, which would make the stomach acid slither up into his throat. Another pill to make the stomach acid go back down. Finally, there was Vicodin for the burning, gnawing foot pain.

Lloyd sometimes fantasized about a magic department store with a LIFE section. He would stroll up to the counter and say something like *"Excuse me. I have been given the wrong life by mistake, and I would like to trade this life in for another one, please."* But there is no magic store and Lloyd slowly came to realize that he would be stuck in his broken down, painful body until that creepy fellow with the black robe and the sickle finally paid him a visit.

* * *

Sunday was intensely bright, with a merciless sun that seemed hell bent on punishing all who lie beneath it. Lloyd had been up late the night before binge watching The Andy Griffith Show on Netflix. Don Knotts was so funny when his humongous balloon eyes bulged with excitement.

After a lonely breakfast consisting of Raisin Bran and coffee, Lloyd settled his ass squarely into his Tommy Bahama chair on his front lawn and gripped an ice cold can of Guinness--the best damn beer in the history of the world.

The tan house across the street sat eerily still in the warm breeze. It had been vacant for about six months, ever since the Nelsons defaulted on their mortgage and scrammed off to Idaho. Lloyd sat and watched car after car pull up to the Nelsons's old house. Old folks made their way up the front porch, where they were greeted at the door by a dark figure Lloyd could not quite make out. The old timers entered the tan house in a steady stream, one octogenarian after another. By 2 PM there must have been 20 cars parked out front.

Lloyd polished off a few more cans of glorious, milky Guinness. His head was swimming in the type of confidence and lies that only alcohol can manufacture. Lloyd creaked up from his chair and made his way across the street, toward the tan house. He approached the front door, knocked twice, and waited with his hands rustling in his pockets.

Low rumblings were heard in the background. Lloyd noticed the handle twist, as the door slowly swung open. An elderly woman wearing a peach Mumu and excessive turquoise jewelry said, "Why hello, there. We were all hoping you would join us." Her eyes were black and void of life, but Lloyd found them to be quite calming.

The elderly woman gracefully caressed Lloyd's hand and elbow and led him inside. A Wurlitzer jukebox in the corner played Frankie Vallie's *"Can't Take My Eyes Off of You."* The house was full of elderly folks chatting away about things like baseball, grandkids, and BBQ cookouts. Lloyd stood there for a few minutes just watching everyone. A wrinkled, deflated man slowly and deliberately shuffled over to Lloyd with a walker, placing a frail arm gently around Lloyd's shoulders.

"Don't be shy. Tell us about Connie and your beautiful family," said the old man, with a twinkle in his eye.

Lloyd hesitated a moment, then started right in. He told them about Connie going into labor with their daughter at the Angel's game in 1969, and about the time the neighbor's dog ate his son's hamster.

The old timers all shared similar stories, and laughed and cried together through the afternoon. After a while, Lloyd noticed that everyone in his group started to look hollow and transparent. Lloyd saw that his own hands were fading, as well. The old timers continued sharing stories and enjoying each other's company, as a tremendous white force overtook them all.

Hi, I'm Jodie

THE LAST MEMORY Dave had of single life was dancing the funky chicken at a disco in Newport Beach in 1980, with a gold medallion swinging to and fro across his hairy chest. Four kids and two divorces later, Dave remembered those Newport Beach disco days quite fondly. But then again, all that booger sugar he snorted up his nose during those hazy years made it hard to remember much of anything.

Dave's oldest daughter, Traci, had bought him a laptop and taught him how to use the internet. Traci set Dave up with an email account and written instructions on how to use an online dating website.

"It's time to get back out there and meet someone new, Dad. You can't just loaf around the house and eat Hungry Man TV dinners and watch Colombo reruns until you croak," said Traci.

Dave finally decided to give online dating a shot. He sat down in front of his laptop and stared a while at the blinking cursor. *I'd might as well just be honest and say what I'm looking for.*

"Hi, I'm Dave. I'm looking for a gal who is kind and smart, and who won't hassle me about leaving the toilet seat

up, because I like leaving it up and I'm never going to change my mind about that. Also, I hate technology. People who stare at their smart phones all day are losers. If you have a smart phone and look at it all the time and if you have a Facebook account, I am going to assume you are not a very nice person so please don't contact me. I also don't send text messages, because I have a voice, and I speak very well. Text messages are for mutes, so if you ever need to contact me, just call me on the telephone, or drive over to my house and knock on the front door for Pete's sake! I also don't like navigation devices in cars, because I don't like some robot-broad nagging me every time I need to make a left turn. I just like to use my trusty map book, which has been getting me around just fine since 1973. That's all.

* * *

Four days later, Dave received a telephone call from a lady with a nice, soothing voice.

"Hi, is this Dave? My name is Jodie. I saw your personal ad on the dating website. Can we meet tomorrow for lunch? There's this great diner in Mission Viejo on Crown Valley Parkway."

"Sure honey, let's meet there at noon."

* * *

Dave casually breezed through the front door of The Filling Station Diner at 11:20 AM the following morning. He got there early to secure a comfy booth with padded seats, because hard wooden chairs made his ass sore and caused his balls to ache. Dave gulped down two cups of hot coffee and polished off a hearty piece of apple pie with some vanilla ice cream. *Just so I'm not meeting this gal on an empty stomach.*

Jodie made her entrance into The Filling Station at noon sharp, swiveling her head to the right, then to the left. Dave saw her immediately and waived, pleased by her attractive appearance and her promptness. Jodie looked about 55. She was well put together, too. It looked as though she kept herself in pretty damn good shape. Good teeth, good hair, nice clothes, and a friendly smile.

"Hi there, Jodi, I'm Dave. Well, I guess you already know that. It's great to meet you."

"I'm glad were meeting here. I love diners, and this place has got just about the best pancakes in Orange County," said Jodi.

Dave was too old and too impatient to waste any time.

"Can you tell me a little bit about yourself, Jodi?"

"Well, let's see. I like long walks on the beach, but usually by myself. If I'm walking with someone else they often annoy me with their comments and ramblings. I just like to walk, and listen to the ocean's waves gently slap against the shore. I like dogs, but not those little snippy dogs. I've been divorced five times, and all of my ex-husbands are assholes, without exception. I have three grown children, but I do not speak with any of them. I may have grandchildren, but I'm not sure. I was living in San Francisco in the 1960s and I was recruited into a commune, which turned out to be a cult. I practiced witchcraft throughout most of my twenties and I even pledged my allegiance to Satan while I was wrapped up in all of that. Those days are behind me now, but I still practice witchcraft when there is a full moon. Sometimes I steal things for fun. You know, little things from the corner liquor store—a Mr. Goodbar here, a Slim Jim there. Every once in a while I'll walk into a shoe store, and just walk out through the front door wearing a new pair of shoes without paying for them."

Dave looked at the table, where Jodi's folded hands rested calmly.

"I notice that you don't have a phone with you," said Dave.

"I'm not much of an Internet person. I don't even own a cell phone. I just have a landline, if you can believe that. I guess that makes me sort of a fossil these days," replied Jodi, blushing.

Dave reached across the table and gently took hold of Jodi's hands, squeezing them warmly while gazing into her hazel eyes.

"Baby, I think this is the start of something great."

She Comes In Darkness

I THOUGHT THE HOUSE WAS UGLY, but I bought it anyway. Actually, ugly is not the right word. Awkward is more like it. I bought the house to impress a girl, if you must know.

The girl's name is Becky. Becky likes all of that dark, twisted nonsense—goth music, horror movies, black lipstick, and the like. So I bought this big ugly (I mean awkward) house to impress Becky. I suppose the house is Victorian. It even has one of those "widow's watch" thingamajigs above the roof.

I slept the first night in my new house alone. Becky wasn't there because she was having a "girls' night out" with her twin-bitch sisters. They are identical twins. When I have to stare at their clone-bland faces and their four dreary brown eyeballs I wish I could magically create a trap door in the ground so I could disappear into the earth's crust forever.

Every house seems haunted when you spend your first night under its roof. New or old, it doesn't matter. Every house has a soul, and that soul is trying to decide what exactly it wants to do with you, the newcomer.

This house had a brightness that was mighty offensive. Light would always find a way to shine through the walls, regardless of the night's powerful darkness. That first night, I turned off the lights, shut the curtains, and lay in bed. A harsh uneasiness quickly gripped my insides. The brightness appeared like a lightning bolt ripping through ice water, flooding under the bedroom door and seeping straight through the drywall.

Eventually the brightness faded just a bit and I drifted into a deep sleep. Hours later, I opened my eyes. I was neither awake nor asleep. I was just there, unable to move and physically mummified. My body wasn't just paralyzed, it was completely numb from the tip of my bald head down to my toenails.

That's when SHE appeared: a lovely young woman with long red hair and pale, buttery skin. She held an empty black picture frame inches from my face. "Watch," SHE whispered with peppermint breath and a sinister sneer.

I watched an image of my elderly self, with gray hair and a cane, shuffling through an empty park covered in winter's dead grass. A folded copy of the New York Times stuck out of my back pocket (somehow newspapers managed to survive our technology apocalypse). I grimaced in pain with each movement, and there was a noticeable hunch rounding out the back of my torn sweater. I slowly sat down on a bench, alone, feeding stale bread crumbs to aggressive geese.

By the end of the twenty second preview of what my life was to become, tears were streaming down my face and my mouth had formed into the shape of a pine knot hiding within a dying tree. I had no idea what to make of my future, pitiful self.

SHE disappeared quicker than a handful of talcum powder in the desert wind, and I never saw her again.

The Apostrophe Enforcer

HEY THERE COUNSELOR, do you mind if I smoke? Well I'm going to smoke anyway, if you don't mind. Who wants to live in a country where a man can't enjoy a cigarette and relax at the end of a work day? I'll just use this coffee cup here as an ashtray, thank you very much.

My wife told me the other day that Dana Point is now a "smoke-free city," so now you can't smoke anywhere in town except in your own house. Can you believe that? Those goddamn hippy bastards with their Birkenstocks and Hacky Sacks telling the rest of us how to live our lives! Anyway, I'll cut to the quick.

I've been walking past your law office every weekday for eight years because I get my two donuts every morning at Wally's Donuts on the corner right next to the liquor store owned by the fella with the red dot on his forehead. Glazed donuts are my favorite, but I enjoy an occasional apple fritter or bear claw just as much as the next guy. Those tiny "donut holes" they started selling when Clinton was in office are a complete scam because if you add up the amount of donut you get for the price, you're getting way less donut for your money.

Any who, I need some legal advice so that's why I am sitting across from you in this uncomfortable office chair on a miserably hot August afternoon. Is it true that the attorney/client privilege applies to any discussion that we'll have during this consultation? Is it also true that the attorney/client privilege will prevent you from talking about anything that we discuss here today, unless I tell you that I am going to hurt someone in the future? Great, that's what I thought.

I'm no John Gotti, but I've done a few things that could put me in the slammer. But don't worry, I won't do it again, so your mouth will need to remain shut like a rat trap until the day the undertaker buries you deep in the earth and gives the earthworms the green light to have themselves a nice little lawyer buffet. Some people prefer to be cremated because it's cheaper, but not me. I want to be buried in a nice plush coffin with red velvet inside, with a giant white fluffy pillow to cradle my dead head. Life is long and hard and mean and exhausting and I'll need a long peaceful rest when I reach the finish line. I want to lie under a tree in the shade with birds chirping and leaves blowing in the wind.

Where was I? Oh yea, I did some bad things and I need your help.

Look, I never went to no fancy Ivy League college. In fact, I never went to college at all. I've been working for a living since I was sixteen. But my Aunt Nora was a grammar school teacher, you see. I went to Aunt Nora's house every day after school and she taught me reading, writing, and arithmetic. But most of all, Aunt Nora taught me good grammar. You know, where to put apostrophes, and such. She drilled it into my head so good that I could never forget it. I don't care how smart or educated a man is, if he can't write well and use proper grammar, he ain't shit!

Sometimes a man puts up with a thing in life, until he just can't put up with it no more. That's what happened with me and business signs that are missing apostrophes. One day I was driving down the road minding my own business, and what did I see? A big old whopper of a sign that read "GRAND OPENING—JENNYS CAFÉ."

I stopped my car at a red light and stared with my jaw agape, not believing my eyes. Neither Jenny nor the numb nuts sign maker happened to notice that the apostrophe was missing between the Y and S. The problem is that the sign is telling the public that multiple Jennys owned the café, which is just a bald-faced lie.

So, I pulled into the parking lot, went inside the café, and asked to see the owner. Well, if Jenny herself didn't appear before me in the flesh. She was wearing a pink waitress uniform with a white apron, and she even had a little white hat poking up out of her poufy red hair. She looked like the waitress named Flo from that old TV show "Mel's Diner."

I said "Your sign isn't right. You need to have an apostrophe in your name."

Jenny looked right past me with this confused look on her face.

"What do you mean?" she asked.

I explained to her the best I could why the apostrophe was needed between the Y and the S to show that she, the one and only Jenny, owned the café. Jenny gazed at me and turned her head a little bit to the right, the way a dog does when it hears a high-pitched squeal. I eventually figured that I wasn't going to get anywhere trying to explain highfalutin rules of grammar to some half wit waitress at a café, so I scrammed.

That night I lied in bed tossing and turning. I couldn't think of anything but that stupid sign made by a moron sign maker for a dullard café owner. Sometimes in life you have to take matters into your own hands, so that's what I did. I loaded my pickup truck with my aluminum ladder, a bucket of black paint, and an old paintbrush I had out back in my shed. I drove to the café at about two AM, and the coast was clear. I climbed up on that ladder, dipped the brush deep in the bucket of paint, and slapped that gosh darn apostrophe where it belonged between the Y and the S, once and for all.

"That's more like it," is what I said out loud to myself when I was done.

Right about then, I heard the sound of rubber crushing tiny pieces of gravel on asphalt. I turned around and saw a police car slowly coming to a stop behind me. This skinny little guy, couldn't have been more than twenty years old with pimples covering his face, wiggles his skinny ass out of the patrol car. This guy was so tiny, his gold police badge covered about half of his chest.

The baby cop asked me what I was doing, and I made up some story about how the owner of the joint paid me to fix the sign. He told me that I couldn't be out there that late, and I said no problem, because I was just leaving.

I was driving by Jenny's Café a few days later to admire my handy work, when I noticed that some asshole (probably Jenny herself) had crawled up there and erased my beautiful apostrophe—slapped some white paint right over it. I had tried my best to help that dunce Jenny, but that was the final straw. No more Mr. Nice Guy!

Ever since I was a little boy, I was taught to count to ten when I got mad. Or maybe it was count backwards from ten. I tried to wait a couple days to see if I would feel better about Jenny's sign, but I just couldn't help myself. That same night I drove back to the Café with two gallons of gasoline, a few old rags, and a box of matches. I busted the front window with the metal gas container, poured gasoline around the entrance, lit the rags, and threw the rags and gas containers inside through the broken window. Then I stood there with my arms folded and my feet set in a wide stance in the parking lot and watched the joint light up like a Viking funeral. The flames dazzled and hypnotized me, but I soon snapped out of it and realized that I needed to get the hell out of there before Barney Fife showed up again in his little police costume. I raced out of the parking lot and made a clean getaway before the fuzz arrived.

Here's one thousand dollars cash. I know it's not a lot, but you're not going to have to do much. If the cops want to talk to me, I'll tell them that they need to talk to my lawyer. All you need to do is tell the cops that you don't know nothin' about nothin'. Maybe also tell them that if they had any damn sense they would be investigating Jenny for arson and insurance fraud.

By the way, I noticed that the sign on your door says "Law Offices," followed by your name. It looks to me like it's just you all alone here in this single office. You don't have multiple offices like your sign says, do you? Hell, you don't even have a secretary!

How do you explain your false advertising, counselor?

Harold's Great Escape

HAROLD WAS ENJOYING a well deserved snooze on the couch on a Sunday afternoon. A light breeze fluttered across the top of his feet and gently rustled the hairs of his forearms.

HARRYYYYYYYYY, are you gonna take out the trash or just lie there like a bum!!! My God, how that woman could scream. Her voice was where boners went to die. But Janice's nagging was the least of it.

After 25 years of marriage, Janice still insisted on calling him Harry. Harold hated being called Harry, mostly because Clint Eastwood's character in the Dirty Harry movies was such a ridiculously macho douche, and also because Harold actually was quite hairy. Calling him Harry just made his unattractive furry affliction more obvious to all within earshot.

Harold spent many nights fantasizing about hopping on a Greyhound bus with a one-way ticket to Nowheresville, USA, where the screaming monster with black chin whiskers would never find him. Maybe he could meet a kind woman who would call him by his Christian name and cook cornbread and chicken pot pies for Sunday night dinner.

But Janice had convinced Harold that if he ever tried to leave her, she would find him and drag him back home, gripping him by his nuts if necessary. *"We're Catholics, Harry, and don't you forget it. Catholics are married for LIFE, not like those Episcopalian kooks."*

Many years back, when Janice was more youthful and less arthritic, some unfortunate soul made the mistake of crashing a car into the side of her Nissan as she was pulling out of the parking lot at the Piggly Wiggly. Janice exited her vehicle, popped the trunk, and emerged into the blazing sun wielding a tire iron. The driver stepped on the gas and tried to getaway. Janice got back into her tiny Nissan and chased the driver through four cities before finally cornering him in an alley. Janice sprang out of her Nissan like a portly superhero, smashed all of the windows and the hood, then dragged the poor bastard from his car and beat him so badly that he never fully regained his ability to speak.

A one-way Greyhound ticket to Nowheresville, USA was not a real plan for Harold.

* * *

Harold had always been amazed by watching magicians perform on TV. But even as a boy, he knew deep down that the magic "tricks" were really just illusions performed by highly skilled showmen. Just like he knew that Hulk Hogan could never really beat Andre the Giant unless wrestling was fake.

But no matter how rational people think they are, they all still want to believe.

Harold was flipping through some channels on a Tuesday

night, when he stumbled upon a David Blaine magic special. David Blaine was attempting to set the world record for holding his breath underwater.

"Oh Jesus Christ Harry, why are you watching that moronic magic show? What are you, eight years old?" said Janice.

"I don't think this is a trick. This guy is actually trying to set the world record for holding his breath underwater," replied Harold.

"Whatever you say, genius. I'm going to Tina's house to watch American Idol."

"Okay honey, have fun," said Harold. The door slammed before he finished his sentence.

Harold found himself immediately mesmerized by David Blaine's dark, mysterious gaze and his serious demeanor that was bordering on a vaudeville routine. *Is this guy putting on an act, or is he for real?* David Blaine was preparing to submerge himself into a massive round water bowl with a miniature opening at the top. He would attempt to sink into the water bowl and break the world record by holding his breath for more than 17 minutes. *17 minutes, good lord!*

Before the big stunt, there were interviews with fitness trainers and other folks who had helped David Blaine train his body to survive such a long time without oxygen. Harold giggled to himself as he watched a frail little Indian man explain the process.

"Vut vee did vuz show Daveed how to slooooow his beating heart. Slow heart means less oxeeegin is needed for da body. I tell David to veelax and tink of da nice tings he has seen and da nice places he has been. Tink of a beautiful vooman if it helps to veelax da mind. It is the mind over the matter, yes it is."

Harold enjoyed the next 20 minutes of this new American pastime—watching the physical suffering of others from the comfort of your La-Z-Boy chair. David Blaine floated in the water lifelessly with his limp arms hanging at his sides. *What is a good looking, muscular young fellow like David Blaine doing floating around in a goddamn fishbowl with no air to breathe? If I were him, I'd be out on the town chasing skirts.*

David Blaine finally emerged from the fishbowl looking halfway dead, shaking like some poor epileptic geezer. But he did it. He broke that dumb world record for lasting the longest amount of time without breathing air.

* * *

Sometimes in life a man develops a vision over a period of weeks, months, and even years. Like opening a business or training for a marathon. Other times, a man gets struck by an idea so hard and fast that it feels like a lightning bolt pierced right through one side of his skull and out the other.

Harold sat there watching David Blaine defy the laws of nature, and was stunned by his own revelation. He would escape Janice for good, and she would never find him.

* * *

Harold waited until Janice ran down to the Piggly Wiggly to grab a pack of cigarettes. Kools, that was her brand.

When they had first met at the age of 19, Harold thought that wafty menthol smell was kind of sexy, the way it clung to Janice's hair and clothes like a wet piece of Saran Wrap. Looking back, Harold realized that he only thought that putrid faux minty smell was sexy because he thought Janice was a hot little number in her own sloppy, Woodstock kind of way.

Boy, were those days gone forever.

Harold's first trial run of his brilliant escape plan was not very encouraging. With Janice out of the house for at least 20 minutes, Harold lied stiff as a corpse on his bed, pressed the timer button on his Iron Man watch, forced a deep breath into his diaphragm, and tried not to breathe. The first 20 seconds were actually quite relaxing. Then the agony began. Harold felt as if every cell in his body were begging him to do something that he needed to do, but that he was stubbornly refusing the loud sirens of nature.

After springing from his pillow like a Jack-In-the-Box and taking a dramatic gasp for oxygen, Harold focused his eyeballs on his Iron Man watch. 44 seconds, that was it. He had a long way to go, but he knew what was at stake. Practice, practice, practice. Every day, no exceptions.

Each night after Janice went to bed, Harold would lie down on the couch, slow his breathing, and hold his breath for as long as possible. He even practiced holding his breath when he was walking around the house, running errands, doing yard work, and washing dishes and cleaning up the kitchen. Since Janice never spoke to Harold, she didn't seem to notice his new found silence.

Slowing down his heart was the next step. Harold committed to meditation and centered his entire existence around calming himself down and slowing his heart rate. Every time Janice would yell at him, Harold would close his eyes and think about that trip he took with his family to Maui as a teenager. Nothing but pineapple juice, the hot sun, waves, and babes in bikinis. *Breathe, breathe, breathe. Slow, slow, slow. Babes in bikinis.*

After six months of training, Harold could hold his breath for five minutes. If he really focused, he could slow his heart rate down to 20 beats per minute, maybe even a little bit lower.

It was time to go for it.

* * *

Janice was in the kitchen, cooking one of her Hamburger Helper "cancer casseroles," as Harold liked to call them. Harold positioned himself on the couch as he had planned for weeks, and started taking deep, slow, deliberate breaths. *Deep breaths, relaxing thoughts.*

"Harry! Get your ass in the kitchen and make some vegetables and clean the casserole dish."

Harold reached into his right front pocket and pulled out two large Alka-Seltzer tablets. He placed both of them into his mouth, and took a sip of water. He then took three tremendously deep breaths, and held the last one in his diaphragm. Foam grew in his mouth like a white bubbly spider with a billion legs, then escaped through his slightly parted pink lips.

"Are you deaf or what?" Janice said entering the family room. "Harry, are you sleeping again? Oh my God, Harry wake up!"

Janice ran to the couch and kneeled by Harold's side, wiping the foam from his lips. Harold's heart rate had slowed so much and he was in such a deep meditation that it seemed as if Janice was yelling at him from another dimension. When she ran to the kitchen to grab the phone, Harold briefly opened his eyes and took a series of desperate deep breaths. When he heard Janice coming back into the room, he took an incredibly deep breath into his diaphragm, and held it.

"I think my husband's had a heart attack. Send an ambulance now, and don't lollygag!"

Harold needed to seriously slow his heart before the ambulance arrived. He thought about the trip to Maui again. He thought about the great girls he had met before Janice wrecked his life. *Deep, slow breaths.*

It's hard to say how much time passed, but Harold had entered another universe by the time a cluster of firefighters had raced through the front door. *Maybe I really am dead.* There were distant discussions about a code blue, epinephrine, and a defibrillator. Harold felt a pinprick, then a shock to his chest, but he just kept on dreaming about Maui. And babes in bikinis.

I cannot spend another day with Janice. David Blaine did it and I can do it too.

* * *

When Harold awoke, he was cold and naked. And alone. The room was bright but drab, and a little tag was hanging from his left big toe. He was sprawled out on a table surrounded by corpses, most of them old and wrinkled. *I did it, they all think I'm dead!*

But he would not be alone for long. Murmurs could be heard in the hallway of the morgue.

Harold ripped the toe tag off his left big toe and stepped down from the cold steel table. The frigid air felt hostile against his naked skin. Harold looked through a small window over the cadaver table, and saw that the night sky was as black as tar.

This would be his only chance.

Harold's feet apparently made his decision for him, as one naked foot after the other pranced with intense purpose toward the double doors at the back of the autopsy room. Harold's arms were apparently in agreement with his feet, as he watched them fling open the doors and whip back and forth against his body as he sprinted toward a corn field behind the coroner's building.

Harold ran like he had never ran before, with his manhood slapping against his thighs and his long grey hair flowing in the warm summer breeze. He had no plan, except to live a life worth living.

And to never smell another Kool cigarette again.

Handle With Care

"I WANT TO THANK everyone for braving the heat today and helping us celebrate another glorious year at the Orange County Fair. Be sure to check out Pat Benatar and Joan Jett tonight on the Main Stage at 8 o'clock. Without further ado, please help me give a warm welcome to real life snake handlers from Christ the Redeemer Pentecostal Church. These folks traveled all the way from Kentucky to be here with us today, so please help me give a warm welcome to Gus and Genevieve."

A tall, gaunt man with alabaster skin accented with freckles made his way to the microphone. Gus was a frail man who had no business growing a beard, though he tried anyway. His face was covered with weak, curly red hair that left empty patches of boy-like skin exposed along his cheeks and neck. By the looks of Gus, most people would suspect that he lived a foul, hard-drinking life, and they would be right.

"Hello everybody, my name is Gus. I have been the proud pastor at Christ the Redeemer Pentecostal Church since 1984. I stand before you as a humble servant of the Lord. This here is my lovely wife, Genevieve. By a show of hands, how many

of you believe in our Lord and Savior Jesus Christ? For those
of you who did not raise your hands just now, maybe we will
help to change your mind by what we are about to show you
here today."

Genevieve walked toward stage left carrying six glass tanks, placing them at Gus's feet at the front of the stage.

"These are venomous rattlesnakes. They have not been
tampered with in any way, and they all still have their fangs.
The Lord tells us in the Holy Bible that we are to handle
venomous and dangerous creatures, and that He will protect
us," said Gus.

Genevieve stood a few feet to the right of Gus, stoically admiring his presence. Her black and gray hair ran well past her shoulders, coming to an uninspiring finale at her mid back. Deep creases invaded her face from top to bottom, revealing a rough life and an even rougher marriage. Genevieve was a large woman with large breasts. In her youth, she wore the most conservative dresses she could find to avoid the uninvited stares of men. Eventually, Genevieve learned that men were going to stare at her fleshy mounds regardless of what she wore, so around middle age she decided to give the men a show if that's what they wanted. On this day, she proudly wore a flowery low cut top that left little to the imagination.

Gus dramatically rolled up his dirty white sleeves, then slowly lowered his right hand into one of the tanks, retrieving a beat up, skinny looking brown snake. The spectators in the first few rows could hear the rattles hissing like a car tire that had sprung a leak. Those same people could also clearly see the empty swath of air where Gus's right middle finger should have been on his crooked and weak looking hand.

Gus closed his eyes and gazed his face straight up toward the sky. His lizard skin boots shuffled and tapped across the stage, kind of like James Brown at the Apollo, only slower and more methodical. *Scoot, scoot, scoot—shuffle, shuffle, shuffle.*

Gus made his way over to the next tank, and pulled out another rattler. This one wrapped itself around Gus's neck, creating a diabolical, scaly necklace. Gus kept shuffling and dancing his way around the stage, picking up snake after snake, until he looked like a cross between Medusa and a used car salesman sporting a cheap suit. The crowd gasped with horror and curiosity. A little boy wearing red cowboy boots chewed his fingernails to the quick and drew blood. A young girl with blonde pigtails and yellow overalls clasped a hand over a wide open mouth full of missing teeth.

Genevieve grabbed the microphone from the stand, walked over to Gus, and held the microphone up to his mouth. His eyes were still closed, as he performed his little shuffle-dance for the crowd.

Then the strangest of sounds echoed through the fairgrounds.

"blacka mu chaka mu mamba mabay. Lala bu mancha lalalalalala bubububu seeee chikow!" Gus was speaking in

tongues.

Most of the audience members would have scoffed at the absurd soundbites pouring from Gus's mouth, were he not covered head to toe in deadly snakes. Gus gave the appearance of a man possessed, and perhaps he was.

* * *

Snakes hold a secret as old as the universe. They communicate with one another through their eyes. Even in the dark, when snakes lock eyes they can see deep into each other's soul and feel happiness as well as torment. Snakes are patient and meticulous planners, too.

The drive from Kentucky to California had been brutal for the snakes. Stuck in tiny cages in the back of Gus's dirty old van for more days than the snakes could count, they started plotting their revenge. The snakes had played along as pathetic props at Gus and Genevieve's old Kentucky church for long enough. The unsympathetic heat from the still and windless summer day at the Orange County Fair had been the final straw.

* * *

As Gus pranced around the stage with his eyes rolled deep into his skull, Genevieve clapped her hands enthusiastically as she stood just one foot away, acting as a one-woman cheerleading squad. The snake in Gus's left hand stared intently into the eyes of a snake anchored around Gus's neck. *Let the bitch have it first.* A third snake coiled snugly on top of Gus's head responded: *Just say when.*

Genevieve faced Gus, again moving the microphone to his face so the audience could hear him speak in tongues. With a sudden jolt, the first two snakes leaped from Gus, simultaneously sinking needle-sharp fangs into Genevieve's breasts. Genevieve looked down, and her artificial smile melted into the most miserable of grimaces. Her mouth opened wide enough for her to fit her entire fist, as an ear piercing shriek blasted from her throat. A third snake lunged from the top of Gus's head and forced its fangs straight through Genevieve's tongue.

Genevieve stood on stage with her feet planted sternly on the wooden floor and her arms spread wide. Three scaly ropes violently twitched and swerved to the left, to the right, then up, down, and in twisty circles. Before Gus realized what was happening, Genevieve crumpled onto the stage as a fleshy heap of meat and bones.

Three snakes smoothly slithered from Genevieve's body, forming a neat line at the front of the stage. Gus stood there staring at Genevieve, as his face twisted in terror and slow-motion surprise. As he stared blankly into the crowd, the head of a rattlesnake blocked his view just before biting him right on the forehead. Gus crumpled onto the stage clutching his face as the two remaining rattlers took hold of his neck tightly, injecting him with hot white death. The heels of Gus's old lizard skin boots kicked and scratched the stage a few times, then Gus made his long-awaited departure from our universe.

The six rattlers faced the cluster of shocked children, cigarette smoke, and dropped clumps of cotton candy. In unison, the snakes shot like hot poisonous arrows from the stage, onto the ground, moving quickly through stampeding waves of Converse and Birkenstocks. A few of the snakes stopped to feast on dropped pieces of corn on the cob and over-sized, steroid-infused turkey legs, but mostly they just kept moving.

If they could make it into the surrounding brush, they could hide out until just before dark. Then they would slide their way into the quiet suburbs, full of unsuspecting inhabitants and plump rodents. Never again would a human handle these snakes and live to tell the tale.

The Trail's End

EVEN THE WRETCHED have children, thought Jean, as she sauntered at a brisk pace past a pregnant hobo lying on the walking trail, adjacent to her glass tower high rise office building. Jean often wondered from where these faceless, anonymous members of society originated. It was easy to forget that the homeless were actually people, but Jean was too preoccupied with the vapid details of her own petty life to pay much attention to them. She liked to think of herself as a charitable person, but in truth Jean spent more time pondering which Netflix series she would binge-watch next than she did pondering the fate of the endless rows of homeless that ruined an otherwise beautiful walking trail.

There was a time when Jean made valiant efforts to convince herself that she braved the homeless each weekday at noon because daily exercise was an important part of a healthy lifestyle. But as Jean aged, she lost the energy necessary to convince herself of such fantasy. The truth was that Jean walked quickly with her elbows flailing every day at lunch time because if not, her ass would become fat. "Chair ass," was what her coworker Tracy called it. And if her ass became fat, Jean would spend her remaining Saturday nights alone with her cat

Velda. So Jean walked, and she walked hard. Every weekday at noon sharp. The trail wound through pine trees and oak trees. Plump squirrels darted back and forth. The lonely elderly were there too, feeding stale peanuts to random, bloated critters.

Jean had slipped off her flats and laced up her New Balance before leaving her desk each day for her two mile trek across the homeless-nature-suburban trail. She had learned to ditch her skirt suits in favor of pantsuits. Jean could get away with dark blue jeans on Thursdays and Fridays, if she wore a smart looking blazer with the right accessories. On this day, Jean wore dark blue jeans, her New Balance, and a thin red sweater, with stupid jingly bracelet accessories, earrings, and a necklace, to show that she was not a slob, and that she put some effort into looking presentable before she left the house.

Jean's face was pretty but not beautiful. As a teenager, she had cute freckles adorning her nose and cheeks, which morphed into somewhat unruly sunspots as she skidded into 40. Jean once read a photojournalism article showing what aging rock stars looked like when they woke up first thing in the morning. The photographer showed up at the musicians' houses at 5 AM, woke them up, and took their picture as they opened the front door. One of the old rocker dudes told the newspaper reporter, *"When you're born, you have the face God gave you. When you're 40, you have the face you deserve."*

Jean was not so sure that she deserved the gobbler chin that had been gradually appearing in her horror-house bathroom mirror each morning, but at least God had allowed her to keep her gorgeous thick mane of blonde hair. Also, her body had not yet completely betrayed her. She still had just enough curves to catch men's attention when walking in public. If she focused on her peripheral vision, Jean could spy quite a few older gentlemen checking out her ass when she wore her black yoga pants. Some women had the roving eye, too.

Jean could not help but sneer just a tad at the men she spotted roaming the halls in their work-a-daddy uniforms consisting of cheap polyester slacks, cheaper synthetic button-down collar plaid shirts, and comfy scuffed leather shoes. Half the time, the slobs didn't even bother to shave before leaving the house. Jean figured that being a man must be like winning the lottery and not having to pay taxes on the loot.

Jean lurched onto the trail alone on this day because everyone else in her office had agreed to be good Samaritans and head over to the Red Cross "Bloodmobile" in the parking lot to donate blood. The sun was intensely bright and the sky was an obnoxious turquoise blue. Jean began at a snail's pace, then picked up speed once her heart started kicking and her lungs came to life. It had been raining like a bastard all month long, and the plants and shrubs were thick and lush.

A radio played music in the distance, and the sounds encroached closer and closer to Jean. A hairy, muscular man sporting a shiny bald head and wearing a food stained tank top shot around the corner on the trail and headed straight toward

Jean, riding a blue Huffy beach cruiser covered in old random bumper stickers. *Where's The Beef?* read a sticker slapped across the handlebars. An old radio was held in place on top of the handlebars by green bungee cords with dead rusty hooks. The man rapidly pedaled the beach cruiser in a manner suggesting he was either running from an intimidating figure, or chasing someone weak. His face was weathered, with a grimace suggesting either physical pain or emotional misery. Maybe both. Jean heard Whitney Houston crooning from the old radio *and IIIIIIIIIIIIIII will always love youuuuuuu!!* Whitney's singing became louder and louder as the beach cruiser approached, then Whitney's voice suddenly became warped and mangled as the smelly man on the bike whipped past her, causing wind to ruffle Jean's hair a just bit.

As Jean hit her stride, she heard whispering coming from no particular direction. She kept walking, wondering if she was maybe hearing things. Sometimes when Jean drank too much coffee in the morning, she would hear things and see things that were not there. Her shrink had suspected early stage schizophrenia and advised Jean to avoid coffee, cannabis, and any other stimulant, but Jean had decided early on that her shrink was a quack because he had a beard that grew all the way down past his ugly Adam's apple. Any diligent professional with an eye for detail would at least take the time in the morning to shave the hair from his pencil neck to make his beard look tidy and presentable.

But the whispering did not stop and the sounds became more intrusive with each step. The paved portion of the trail gave way to loose dirt covered with pine needles and dead leaves. Jean passed through a patch of shade under a massive oak tree, then into the open bright blue sky. The smell of the oak trees always reminded Jean of camping trips she took as a young teenager. The whispering turned into muttered words. A row of massive sunflowers perked up as Jean approached, staring directly into her eyes and following her movements, as if receiving an old friend for dinner. The dirt shuffled and vibrated below Jean's feet and long green vines from the side of the trail took hold of her ankles. Jean looked down, only to notice that the long, dirty green vines had also taken hold of her wrists tightly enough to halt the flow of blood to her hands.

A tremendous force yanked Jean to the Earth. The back of Jean's head was suctioned into the dirt, as the dirty green vines gently caressed her arms and legs. The massive sunflowers approached Jean with a vicious curiosity and leaned into her face. The sun became so bright, that the entire blue sky surrendered to a whiteness so belligerent that Jean could only yelp like a wounded dog in its presence. The flowers and the vines were eager to see Jean close up, but the sun was the most interested of all. The horrendous white orb maneuvered closer and closer to Jean, until she was screaming with madness as she went blind and the horrific brightness became the darkest of all dark.

As the sun asserted its dominion over Jean's entire reality, the heat became so oppressive that sweat splashed from Jean's torso and head, marrying chunks of dirt to her body and hair. The sound of sizzling sweat erupted from Jean's forehead, and her eyeballs liquefied. Jean smelled burning hair, then burning leaves. The heat seemed to melt time away too, as the course of events not only slowed, but became unrecognizable. Jean's own movements and shrieks of pain were deliberate, but seemed to be happening to someone else. The vines holding Jean to the earth made painstaking movements, as if they were covered in wet tar with an outer layer of thick carpet.

The ground opened beneath Jean. She hung suspended over the empty blackness for a lonely brief moment, breathless and carefree and paralyzed with hope. Blasts of steaming and frigid air shot into Jean's back from the depths of the seamless pit. The dirty green vines released Jean's arms and legs with a casual flick, and Jean descended alone into the Earth's deep, hollow universe.

They Want One of Us

THERE WAS NEVER anything wrong with calling a female flight attendant a stewardess, as far as Ray Spencer was concerned.

Ray's flight from John Wayne Airport in Orange County, CA to Boise, Idaho seemed less like a ride on an airplane and more like a bus ride straight into the dirty part of town. You know, that part of town where the green belts in the center of the road suddenly turn brown. The part of town where stray dogs proudly strut along the sidewalk with no owner in sight.

The Internet "airfare wars" were surely to blame for the sad depreciation in the quality of air traveler. Ray remembered the days when people changed out of their pajamas and put on some goddamn shoes and socks before boarding an aircraft. When a woman would board a plane, she would be dressed to the nines in stockings, a skirt suit, with her hair done up like Jackie O. When a dame like that pranced by, Ray would smell Chanel no. 5 up and down the aisle for a nice long while.

Ray looked to his left to witness a disheveled man wearing flip-flops and eating Cheetos while licking orange gooey Cheeto crust from his fingers. The man's bratty brood of kids drew on the back of the seat in front of them with crayons. *Holy Christ.*

The pilot took to the speaker to give a detailed, blow-by-blow commentary about how he would fly the plane and where it was going. *Let me guess, genius. You're going to scoot this hunk of tin up into the air, slap on the autopilot, then waste the next 2 ½ hours jawboning with your co-pilot about how your wife keeps breaking your balls to have more kids. Then you two morons are going to trade notes about which one of the stewardesses is the best in the sack.*

Ray dozed off after his third Stolichnaya on the rocks. After a vivid dream about blue snails and flying checkerboards, Ray peeled his crusty eyes open to the deafening white glare of the midday sun. His tongue was burning from the dryness. Fluffy white clouds passed by like drunken marshmallows wandering the streets of Tijuana at three AM.

The sky quickly grew dark, as if God had lowered the dimmer switch before telling a scary story. It didn't quite look like nighttime, but it would have been dark enough to make the streetlights flick on in Ray's neighborhood.

Ray spied through his window a massive object expanding at least two hundred feet in all directions from the top of the plane. A loud, deep THUMP rolled through the heart of the aircraft. Women screamed, children cried, and men grunted. A woman struggling through the less forgiving part of her forties crossed her chest and started praying. She was holding one of those books from the Oprah Book Club about going to heaven and having a fantastic party with dead relatives.

In the center of the roof, a perfectly round pothole was cut. The circular piece dropped squarely into the aisle. There was much mumbling and finger pointing at the new hole in the center of the roof. There was no suction coming from the hole, just sounds of things bumping and tossing about at the top of the airplane.

A round, living object peeked down through the hole. It was an upside down, oval-shaped head with massive black eyes and a tiny mouth no larger than a piece of Trident chewing gum. The head bobbed and weaved and the face grimaced. The creature was struggling. *The dummy cut a hole that's too small. Now he can't fit his entire body through!*

The head disappeared, then two skinny, pale arms were thrust through the hole. Each hand had just three skinny, long white fingers. The tips of each finger were bulbous, covered with suction cups. The arms and hands were hairless, but were shiny and glistening. *They just want one of us.*

Ray felt himself standing up and walking aimlessly toward the two skinny, shiny hands poking through the hole in the center of the airplane. The hands could sense Ray's movements. A single finger started to motion toward Ray, enticing him to keep taking steps forward. Ray followed the motions of his feet without any questioning or doubt.

Ray stopped abruptly once he reached the hole. Three slimy fingers gently caressed the top of his skull, making their way down to his forehead, eyes, nose, nostrils, and lips. The middle finger passed back and forth along Ray's lips over and over again, before entering his mouth and massaging his tongue and teeth. The fingers made their way down to Ray's neck, where they gently massaged the muscles and ligaments around his spine. Ray found himself becoming increasingly dizzy and sleepy.

The three fingers seized control of Ray's head with a firm and determined grip. Ray felt himself moving up toward the hole in the ceiling, noticing that his feet were no longer touching the ground. A warm, buzzing sensation cascaded over Ray from head to toe, distracting him from the blinding bright white lights hovering over the airplane.

Maybe it won't be so bad once I get to where they're taking me. Maybe folks will be nice there. Maybe the aliens will worship me like some sort of God from the far reaches of the universe. Maybe everyone on their planet has tiny little brains, and I will be able to assert control over them with my superior human intelligence. Maybe I can become King of the Dummies.

Drifting

TWENTY FOUR MILES does not seem like a great distance when you are staring hard into the ocean's heartlessness.

On a clear day, Toby could see the entire outline of Catalina Island, including the mountain peaks and the nadir near the middle. While waiting for a new set of waves to roll in, Toby would straddle his longboard with his legs circling in the water to keep his balance, and gaze out over the gleaming sun-specked water toward that long, clunky mysterious looking hunk of rock. He knew plenty about the tourists who visited the island, but he wanted to know who actually LIVED there.

Were the folks who lived there happy? How many plumbers lived on Catalina Island? Was there just one dentist on the island? What if that dentist was not so good with his hands and made people's teeth worse? Could you find another dentist on the island? Do they ever run out of beer on Catalina Island? Do the islanders fight over crucial supplies like toilet paper and bagels? How many police officers live on the island? What if you find yourself stuck on the island with a rogue police officer like Harvey Keitel in that 90's movie The Bad Lieutenant?

The waves at Newport pier were small on this day, and Toby found himself in a sort of trance — gazing at the ocean, with the ocean gazing back at him showing greater intent. Usually when the waves were this small, Toby would pounce down on his longboard and paddle back and forth between the pier and the jetty to get some exercise. Toby didn't consider himself to be old yet, just kind of OLDISH. At least he could say that 30+ years of surfing had kept his shoulders, chest, and arms respectably toned. However, his beer gut was another story, best saved for another day. But there was no exercise paddling on this day, because Toby was just feeling BLAH. Not hung over, not tired, not overworked. No, Toby had just been overcome by a feeling of overall defeat.

Toby didn't know much about boats, but he saw a small white one cruise up past the pier, a bit too close to where the surfers were bobbing up and down in the water like floating bowling pins. The boat sat there in one spot for a while, with the motor idling, making little bubbles pop up at the back of the boat, as if a giant was hiding under water and blowing through a straw.

Before Toby noticed the outline of a human body, he saw glorious, thick blonde hair flapping in the breeze. The unofficial flag of Southern California. Then he saw her. She stood there under the punishing bright sun with golden skin, sparingly covered by a few scraps of a white bikini. Both of her hands were rolled into tight fists, placed unapologetically onto her hips. Oversized dark sunglasses formed a plastic veil over the top half of her face. Although Toby was about 200 feet from the boat, he could see that this was not a woman who was relaxing on a hot summer day. She looked distressed and panicked.

Toby had paddled out a tad bit farther than the other surfers, hoping to catch some of the larger waves coming in that day. She saw Toby, removed her hands from her hips, and waved them over her head while looking directly in Toby's direction. She then held out her right hand toward Toby and motioned for him to paddle closer.

Toby looked around, unsure that he was the intended recipient of her gesture. As it became clear that there was no one else within Toby's immediate vicinity, he looked back at the woman and just stared. She stopped for a moment, placing her hands back at her sides, then resumed her waving and motioning toward the boat.

DOES THIS GIRL WANT TO PARTY OR SOMETHING? HOW CAN SHE TELL WHETHER I'M GOOD LOOKING FROM SO FAR AWAY?

The former Toby was a responsible man who would have looked away and paddled toward shore. Post-divorce Toby, on the other hand, had learned to take more risks in life. Toby's nasty divorce had not only cost him his wife, his kids and his house, but his career as well. At first he had only been drinking at home after work. Eventually, Toby snuck a bottle of Tito's vodka into his office, just to take the edge off in the mornings. He managed to hold everything together until the day he told his boss to "shove a bag of dicks in his ear." Goodbye cushy job in a nice office, hello checkout line at Trader Joe's.

But it wasn't just his job and his wife and the drinking that drove Toby over the edge. His four kids had taken a mighty toll, too. The screaming and yelling and fighting had all become too much. Toby had once believed in a master race of "Super Parents" who could calmly handle the insanity of parenting. Eventually, Toby realized that those Super Parents were frauds who were just faking it when in public. If Mother Teresa and Gandhi had a brood of kids together, it would just be a matter of time before Gandhi was driving in a minivan with the screaming brats in the backseat after a miserable sleepless night. Gandhi would lose his shit and lash out at the kids and Mother Teresa might try to intervene, but it would be hopeless.

Toby had been surfing three days a week since his divorce and he was in pretty damn good shape. He paddled out to the boat in about 60 seconds.

"Hi, I need a hand. Can you please help me? Tie your leash to the ladder and climb on up," said the girl.

Toby climbed onto the boat, dripping wet.

"Hey there. I'm Toby. Do you need help with something."

"I'm Samantha," she said, holding out her hand.

Toby shook her hand, noticing that the boat was spotless. No signs of drinking or eating or anything else that you would expect on a party boat floating off the coast of Newport Beach. There was no sign of anyone else on the boat, which was strange. This was not the type of girl who took up sailing or learned how to do much of anything on her own. She was a party girl. A socialite. Definitely not the lonely sailor type. She was good at smiling and pleasing and entertaining. She maybe had an Associates degree from a community college, but probably not.

She was a looker, though. Damn near 6 feet tall with sun kissed skin covering nothing but hard, toned muscle from head to toe. Perfect feet with professionally manicured nails — the fancy type of manicure where the tips are white. She lifted her glasses onto the top of her head, revealing hypnotizing blue sparkly orbs outlined by enticing dark makeup. Eyes that were beautiful and privileged, but eyes that had never seen a single day of hardship or hard work, for that matter. Nothing awful had ever happened to this blessed woman and nothing ever would.

"Here Toby, have a beer," she said, handing him an ice cold Corona from a red cooler.

Toby popped the cap off the Corona with the bottle opener she handed him, and guzzled the entire bottle without taking a breath. He handed the empty Corona bottle to Samantha, and she popped the top off a new Corona and handed it to him, with a look of slight surprise on her face.

"A bit thirsty, are we?"

"Corona is the best chugging beer," said Toby, wondering if Samantha would be impressed by his beer guzzling skills, or whether she would see him as adolescent and unimpressive.

Samantha slyly moved her hand toward Toby, and gently

rubbed the outside of his upper arm with her delicately manicured fingernails.

"You're in really great shape. Do you surf a lot?"

"Every Monday, Wednesday, and Friday."

Samantha placed her hand on Toby's chest and let it linger there for a few seconds. Toby polished off the second bottle of Corona, and stared out toward the ocean. There it was. That old familiar, warm feeling. Toby felt his problems slowly drift away and he was truly enjoying the hot sun and the cool ocean and the rocking of the boat.

"What kind of music do you like?" asked Samantha.

"I don't know, whatever," replied Toby, glaring at her bikini straps with a strange intensity.

Samantha pranced with graceful, narrow feet toward her phone, which was lying lazily upon a crumpled white and blue striped beach towel. Next to her phone was one of those music speaker thingamabobs that look like a giant Tootsie Roll covered in bee stings. Samantha tapped a few buttons on her phone and suddenly Toby heard the Spin Doctors singing about a couple of princes courting the same young girl.

"Whooohooooo, I love this song!" shrieked Samantha.

Samantha's hands made their way to the back of her neck, as her hips flung themselves from side to side in a violent display of contently arrogant youth. Toby noticed that Samantha wasn't just thin, she was SKINNY. So skinny, in fact, that each side of her torso resembled a full slab of baby back

ribs with no sauce. Toby had a hard time deciding whether or
not so many protruding bones was a sexy feature. But
what WAS sexy was the way Samantha ran her own fingers
through her gorgeous thick mane of hair. And the way she
licked her lips. And the way her strong, bony knees supported
her carelessly rotating hips. And the way her ass resembled two
perfect scoops of vanilla ice cream. And the way her breasts
confidently occupied their own little slice of the universe
without needing any cooperation from any other part of her
body.

This girl had definitely made the rounds. Exactly where,
Toby could not say, but she had been a woman about town in
Newport Beach. Toby could tell by her steely gaze and hard
movements. Whether she had been dumped, beaten,
abandoned, or ripped off, Toby could not tell. But there was
something artificial about Samantha's icy aloofness that made
Toby feel as if he were in the presence of a mannequin or
perhaps a talking robot from an old Twilight Zone episode.

"Come with me down below, I want to show you
something," said Samantha, grabbing Toby's hand with an
uneasiness that partially explained her sweaty palm.

*WELL I GUESS THIS IS IT. I'M GOING TO FIND OUT WHETHER SHE'S AS
WILD AS SHE LOOKS.*

Toby followed Samantha toward the hull of the boat.
Toby's hand had become willfully encapsulated in Samantha's,
and he could not help but notice the sleek design of her bronze
arm. Her skin appeared to be the sun's most proud and

beautiful creation. Even her elbow joint was delicately built out of the most well proportioned bones and cartilage Toby had seen in his forty-nine years.

A harsh sea breeze clumsily splashed a large chunk of hair into Samantha's face, but she managed to maintain her tight gaze upon Toby. Samantha stopped abruptly, blocking the entrance to the hull, facing Toby directly. She approached his mouth with movements as delicate and deliberate as a sniper on a rooftop, before delivering the wettest and softest of kisses while her manicured fingernails gently caressed the back of Toby's head. Toby felt his heart melt into his stomach, as his knees became wobbly and his face tingled with teenage lust.

"I need you to do something for me," whispered Samantha into Toby's ear, with cinnamon breath.

Samantha gazed deep and hard into Toby's eyes as she gently nodded her chin up and down, causing a nearly hypnotized Toby to voluntarily nod in agreement. Samantha then stepped aside, exposing the entrance to the hull.

Toby's face let out a grunt and a dirty puff of air shot from his mouth, while an ugly dizziness seized his head.

Two fat white legs covered in black hair could be seen from the top of the stairs leading down into the hull. A single bare foot was hooked under the third step from the bottom.

"He beat me one time too many. Look here, if you don't believe me," said Samantha, lifting her hair to show Toby the left side of her neck.

Toby did not see anything except a taut neck covered in sun drenched skin.

"Don't worry. He's more dead than Elvis. Here's what we're going to do. We're going to tie his body down with weights and dump him in the ocean halfway between Catalina Island and San Clemente Island. He's too heavy for me to move without your help. No one will be looking for him, because he was the prick of all pricks."

Toby stood motionless, staring at Samantha's flowing hair, not seeing her lips move as she spoke. He then set his gaze upon the hairy white dead legs sticking out from the hull.

"Have you ever heard of Pitcairn's Island? That's where we're headed after we dump old shit bird into the water. Pitcairn's Island is the most remote, tiny little island in the middle of the South Pacific. Less than fifty people live on the island, and not even Columbo could ever find us there. Nothing but waterfalls, coconuts, white sand, and crystal blue water. And me! I think we can make a pretty good team. What do you think? I've got just over seven million dollars in accessible offshore cash accounts."

Samantha inched closer to Toby and placed her hands on his shoulders, massaging gently with the smooth palms of her bony hands. Samantha's eyes creased at the corners, and her brow became hard and determined. Something told Toby that as soon as he helped Samantha dump "old shit bird" into the deep blue sea, he might be next. Except that when it was Toby's turn, Samantha would be smart enough to simply push him off the boat and into the middle of the ocean at least a hundred miles from the nearest island, so she wouldn't need anyone's help dragging him out of the boat. There would be no Pitcairn's Island, no seven million dollars, and no coconuts in paradise. Not for Toby, anyway.

Toby inched his way closer and closer to Samantha, until they were rubbing their pelvises together like a couple of teenagers slow dancing at the Junior Prom. Toby kissed her neck and then her mouth, while squeezing her ass tight with both hands. Samantha closed her eyes and swayed to the mesmerizing sounds of the waves gently slapping against the side of the bow.

"Adios baby, thanks for the Coronas," said Toby, as he jumped overboard, untied his leash from the boat ladder, and plopped his gut onto the thick coat of wax covering his surfboard.

Toby paddled toward shore as leisurely as a lazy Basset Hound at the park on a Sunday afternoon. A nice swell was coming in from the south, and Toby could see some decent size waves rolling in past the pier. The tide was rising, and conditions would be good in less than an hour. Toby was going to surf hard, until his muscles ached and his lungs burned. On the way home, he would stop at In-N-Out Burger and treat himself to a Double-Double cheeseburger with fries and a vanilla milkshake.

You Can Call Him Jake

THEY TOLD ME I could call him "Jake," but that just seemed strange. Jake was just a large and ostentatious oil painting, after all. Hanging there, staring at all of us from his lofty perch in the great room of an old single story ranch style home in Tustin. I had been invited to "The Sanctuary" by my friend Peter, and I was hoping to learn something profound on this cold and rainy February evening.

Jake seemed to emit some sort of ancient wisdom with his hollow and handsome brown eyes. Up there on the wall, Jake was wearing a green Adidas jogging suit with black stripes running down the arms and legs. Bright white leather K-Swiss shoes with no laces covered a pair of stubby, wide feet. Light brown, curly and disheveled hair covered an oddly shaped cranium. The front of Jake's forehead sloped backward, as if the world's strongest hurricane had caught him off guard one day while sailing. The back of Jake's head was flat, leading up to an eventual point at the top of his skull. Upon close inspection, you could tell that Jake paid big bucks for the best hairstylists of his era to create the optical illusion that his head was normally shaped. The front and sides grew long and bushy, while the hair on top was closely cropped.

Of course, I only realized the unusual shape of Jake's skull because I have an obsession with physical symmetry. Eyebrows, lips, nostrils, thumbs, fingernails, toenails, kneecaps, earlobes — they all must be perfectly symmetrical, you see. Otherwise, I will stare at you. Probably not long enough for you to notice, but I will definitely gaze at you and your lopsided body parts until I figure out exactly what needs fixing. My preoccupation with physical symmetry is part of what brought me to The Sanctuary on this damp evening. Constantly noticing the flaws in others is absolutely exhausting, especially for someone with my special aptitude for spotting physical faults from great distances. I had high hopes that the folks at The Sanctuary could help me live a normal life without this peculiar burden.

Anyway, there stood Jake. With his arms folded and his head looking to the right, peering straight into each of our confused souls. In a better era, Jake could have been the fourth member of Run DMC. JAM MASTER JAKE. The look on his face was not necessarily arrogant, but it certainly was not an expression of humility. Jake's face was weathered but not beaten, with lush and perfectly symmetrical aristocratic eyebrows, and a shave so close that one might suspect electrolysis had been involved.

"You've got a friend for life in Jake. A real bro, someone you can always go to for advice, even if he has been dead for 35 years," said Peter, swaying in front of the oil painting with a beaming smile and an intoxicated look in his eyes.

Peter was a true believer in Jake and all things Jake. A small group of Jake's disciples had found Peter at The Beatnik Bar in San Clemente, the day after Valentine's Day. Peter came stumbling out of the bar wailing about Mona, who had dumped him for no reason at all (that's Peter's version of events, anyway). Peter promised that if I could keep an open mind, Jake's disciples could teach me how to "open my eyes to the world" during a series of seminars at The Sanctuary.

"Come on Sam, let's mingle. Just hang loose and let me do the talking. I think you'll like the people here," said Peter.

I slid over to the bar and grabbed a White Russian, just to level myself out. That milky booze went down like velvet butter, and I finally felt ready to meet some new people and hear all about their unique bullshit.

Peter and I flipped to our right and almost smashed into a couple of young ladies, maybe in their early 30s. A brunette and a redhead. One short and the other even shorter. Both of them damn good looking, though. Before I had a chance to start in with the typical small time chat about freeway routes and urban over-development, I scanned the crowd. It was sure a motley looking crew. Old, young, big, small, professional, blue collar, boisterous, and mousy. They had all gathered together in this one little room. It reminded me of the scene from Cable Guy, where Jim Carrey gathered his group of random, rag-tag friends into his buddy's tiny apartment for the wackiest of karaoke jams.

But we all had something in common. Each of us were Searchers. What were we searching for? Most of us didn't know, but we all knew that something had been missing from our lives since forever.

We had about 20 minutes to get a few drinks and chat amongst ourselves before the seminar would begin. "MANEUVERING THROUGH A CHAOTIC WORLD"was tonight's topic. The scheduled speaker was a tenured Humanities professor from Marmalade College. A poster on the wall showed the athletic Humanities professor casually flexing his muscles against a tight blue cotton T-shirt, with a great beaming smile revealing a row of sparkly, shiny white teeth. But the professor's eyes were too intense and somewhat tortured, looking directly at you but not seeing you at all. No one voluntarily smiles *THAT* hard.

A man in a tweed sport coat and a crisp white shirt and a bowtie gently tapped me on the shoulder before handing me a pamphlet full of questions to guide me through the scheduled lecture. *DO YOU LACK MEANING IN YOUR LIFE? DO YOU BELIEVE IN A HIGHER POWER? ARE YOU A SPIRITUAL PERSON? DO YOU WANT MORE OUT OF LIFE? ARE YOU NOT ACHIEVING YOUR FULL POTENTIAL?*

I circled back to the bar to grab another White Russian for myself and a glass of Zinfandel for the short redhead girl. There was Jake again, staring at me from the wall. I gave Jake's eyes a good hard stare this time, as I patiently waited in line for the burnt out middle aged bartender to serve me at the cash bar. Jake's eyes were wrinkled at the corners, but his pupils were as sharp as a razor. The brownness of his eyes appeared weak and fragile, like a mudslide in Laguna Canyon after a heavy rain. The brush strokes just barely captured the tears welling up above Jake's lower eyelids. If you looked close enough, you could almost see trembling at the corners of Jake's eyes. I realized that Jake was horrified — not so much about what life had in store for him, but horrified that others would catch on to his game.

I handed the glass of Zinfandel to the redhead and gently placed my left hand on her back, between her shoulder blades. She was wearing a thin black tank top, and her bare skin felt warm and soft against the palm of my hand. The redhead smiled and tilted her head toward me in a way that told me that she was enjoying my touch. Her shoulder blades rotated lazily under my hand. I slowly moved my mouth toward her right ear and said something clever that made her giggle just a bit. She had these sexy dimples when she laughed that made me feel like I would melt right there in front of everyone.

We finished our drinks and walked out of The Sanctuary, and I drove us gracefully down the wet and winding road.

Shelly's Shake Shack

THE HORIZON WAS CLOUDY, but the sun was hot. So hot, in fact, that the white sand at Huntington Beach was rumored to have boiled the skin right off the feet of a tourist family from Minnesota. But when young kids are having fun in the sun, not even boiling hot sand will stop them.

Little Jamie stood on the firm, wet sand as the whitewash surrounded her ankles and cooled her sunburned feet. She had to kneel down and splash salt water onto her face and head every few minutes to keep from overheating.

Jamie stood there, ankle deep in the cool water, aggressively sipping a banana-strawberry milkshake her brother Taylor had bought her from "Shelly's Shake Shack." Everyone on the beach had been carrying on about the world famous, undeniably delicious, and hypnotizing milkshakes at Shelly's Shake Shack. Jamie enjoyed the milkshake, but was not a fan of the icky Marciano cherry floating atop the whipped cream. A cherry so obnoxiously red violated all laws of nature. Otherwise, Jamie had to admit that it was a damn good milkshake. Perhaps the best she had tasted in her 10 years.

The thick, sweet milkshake had placed Jamie in a trance of sorts, as she stared out into the vast and empty horizon. White sunscreen started to melt off of Jamie's forehead, burning her eyes, and trickling down both sides of her nose. Her one piece Cinderella bathing suit was starting to heat up, and Jamie tried to finish her shake as quickly as possible, so she could dart into the refreshing Pacific Ocean to cool off.

The beach was so crowded that it reminded Jamie of the time her mom took her to Walmart for a "day after Christmas" sale. Beach goers were packed together so tightly that Nerf footballs were flying here and there and everywhere, like the swallows of Capistrano.

As Jamie continued to gaze into the ocean's slightly curved horizon, she saw about 10 of them. Black spots bobbing and weaving just past the place where the waves were breaking. The black spots would shoot up out of the water a foot or two, only two splash back down under the white caps.

"Sea lions!" shouted a little shirtless boy chewing on three pieces of red licorice. The little shirtless boy pointed with his left index finger and hopped from one foot to the other while grinning with bright red lips, as if he were being electrocuted by the wet sand. The black spots turned into slick heads which turned into elongated, shiny wet black bodies slipping through the whitewash. They made their way to shore within 60 seconds.

Then came the sounds — the shrieks, the yelps, the guttural roars shooting from the throats of the ancient, legless sea beasts. Jamie looked to her left and saw hundreds of these creatures landing upon the shore, and to her right there were hundreds more. The yelps and roars overwhelmed everyone on the beach, and adults and children alike slammed the palms of their hands over their ears.

An old gray and crusty sea lion halted to a stop in the sand at Jamie's feet. She stood there petrified, as the sea lion opened its old mouth and rowdily clapped its front flippers together so close to Jamie's nose that she could feel sea spray blast her face. Jamie screamed like she had never screamed before, causing the tiny punching bag at the back or her throat to flip and flap every which way.

The sea lions charged the sand like an angry battalion of allied forces storming the beaches of Normandy. They stampeded over blankets and umbrellas and boogie boards and tents with reckless abandon. One of them smashed into a teenager holding a can of Cactus Cooler. The dark orange liquid flew through the air while glistening against the sun as a sugary rainbow.

The beach turned nearly black, as the slimy bodies galloped and raced higher and higher, onto the dry sand. The screams and cries of the beach goers were drowned out by the stomping of flippers and the honking from the throats of the determined beasts.

A pimple faced teenager working the counter at Shelly's Shake Shack saw them coming and just stood there slack jawed and confused, dropping his iPhone onto the dirty sticky floor next to his blue Converse All-Stars. He tried to race out the back door, but his knees were wobbly and his legs would obey no commands from his brain. The sea beasts were mean and nasty and determined and they headed straight toward the order window at Shelly's Shake Shack.

The first beast to arrive at the Shack leaped from the sand and flew over the sidewalk, then wiggled straight through the order window. They all followed, until the place was filled up like a clown car with honking and roaring and slapping black sea beasts.

A row of pre-ordered milkshakes had already been filled, and the sea beasts slammed their snouts through the top of the paper cups. Vanilla, banana-strawberry, mango, creamsicle, root beer — all the flavors were there, and then some. The sea beasts snorted and chuckled and drank until the milkshakes were empty. Then they found the milkshake mixers and cleaned them out within seconds. A few of the smart ones knew there was much more treasure to be had, and found the king's ransom supply of ice cream in the back freezer. They gorged and licked every ice cream container clean until there was nothing left but a few empty cardboard boxes.

The gang of whiskered sea beasts ate until they could eat no more, then slowly slithered their way back onto the sand. Terrified tourists and locals witnessed the sea lions dragging their bulging guts across the sand, flopping themselves back into the cold Pacific Ocean. There was no more roaring, no more grunting, and certainly no more flapping of flippers. One of the sea lions threw up on the sand, then slapped one of his flippers onto his forehead and leaned back and stared at the sun with a milkshake hangover for the ages.

Little Jamie stood with her feet in the water, watching the last of the swollen sea lions clumsily tumble back into the ocean. She grabbed her sand shovel and bucket and dug a deep hole to search for some big fat sand crabs.

Eat You Up

Monday

THE SMOKY JOY OF A KOOL CIGARETTE is the mother's milk that sustains me every morning when I awaken around 6 AM. If I can't stuff that hot, sweet smoke into my lungs first thing after I open my eyes, there will be problems.

When I woke up this morning at 5:58 AM and reached with my thin fingers for that familiar crinkly package of tobacco sticks, the palm of my hand struck the top of a lonely and empty nightstand with a THUMP. Before I could hit the lights and get to the bottom of things, I sensed a sharp, burning sensation at my toes. There was blood, too. Not like the blood that drenched Sissy Spacek's angelic face in Carrie, but just enough to make my achy toes stick to the crimson-stained white sheets.

I rolled over onto my left shoulder to watch my wife's glowing skin resting elegantly upon her expensive fluffy pillow, as she purred like a kitten with her eyeballs violently darting back and forth beneath her thin and almost transparent eyelids. This was not the first time I had caught her dreaming. I have often wonder what she dreams about, but perhaps it is best not to know.

My wife never drools, but this morning I spied a tiny red speck at the corner of her mouth. She tends to be a bit sloppy when removing her makeup, but this was different. This particular red spec was dark, with a crusty texture, as if she had eaten something the night before and made a total mess of herself.

Tuesday

The days are getting shorter now, as summer is bleeding a slow death, making way for a predictable fall season. Shorter days mean less sunlight, which explains why I slept longer than normal this morning. 6:24 AM is still a respectable time to start one's day, and this time, my Kools were right where they belong. The ritual of extracting the cigarette from the pack, hearing the crinkling of the plastic and the beautiful auditory click of my stainless steel Zippo makes me feel like the world can be a wonderful place, if just for a fleeting moment.

My nose hurts. Really bad. I press the fleshy part of my index and middle fingers of my right hand onto my nose, and I feel wetness. There is also the coppery smell of blood, which explains why the tips of my fingers are now dark red. I race out of bed and rush to the bathroom mirror to learn that the tip of my nose has been bitten clean off. I cannot tell if there are teeth marks on my nose, because there is too much blood. Nevertheless, the tip of my nose is gone, and I don't know where it is.

I look back at my marital bed, and see that it is empty. My wife's side of the bed is perfectly made, with the sheets and covers tucked so fastidiously tight along the borders of the mattress that it is hard to imagine that any person could be comfortable sleeping there. She must be at the gym. Running herself ragged on an elliptical machine, trying harder than ever to make a clean getaway from Father Time.

Wednesday

Sometimes nightmares seem so real that you wake up crying hysterically, wishing that you could just be back in the second grade and come home from school every afternoon to enjoy a snack of milk and cookies while watching Knight Rider reruns.

Last night was one of those nights. I woke up around 4 AM, feeling trapped and suffocated. I had sensed something rolling and shuffling beneath my sheet. I eventually fell back to sleep after waking from the nightmare, but I woke myself up again with my own screams. There had been an intense pressure around my thighs, and my kneecaps felt as if they were going to explode.

I rolled off the side of my bed and tried to place my feet on the floor. At first it felt as if the floor had been taken away. I felt myself free falling, as if I had jumped off the Golden Gate Bridge. The fall felt like it lasted forever, even though I had only been 18 inches above the floor. The stumps at the end of my thighs smacked the hardwood floor, causing my left femur to jab itself into the wood like a javelin stabbing its way through a field of grass.

I eventually managed to drag myself with my hands across the bedroom floor, into the bathroom. I called for my wife, but she was gone — apparently at the gym again, making her abs tighter and tighter until they would start to resemble a tortoise shell. When she gets home from the gym, my wife will need to help me wrap up my stumps and find me a wheelchair so I can run a few errands today.

Thursday

Man, did I get a good night's sleep. Actually, it felt more like time travel than sleep. I closed my eyes at 9:30 PM, and when I opened them again, it was 6:01 AM.
Some folks are yawners, and some are not. I myself like to greet each new day with a hearty yawn — the kind of yawn that makes your ears pop and gives your jaw a good yoga session. Before reaching for my Kools, I let out a righteous yawn while trying to stretch my arms above my head.

But something was wrong. An empty hollowness sat where my arms used to be. As I tried to reach upward, something warm and slick slipped across my cheeks.
I knew she would do this, that evil bitch. She knew that I would be basically useless without at least having my arms, but that's exactly the type of person she is.

I managed to tumble off the bed and squirm my way to the open door of our bedroom. I screamed her name, but she had already gone. Where she had gone, I did not know.

Our calico cat, Jane, approached me with great stealth. Jane shot a quizzical stare at me, then she got closer. NO, NO, NO! Then the licking started. Jane couldn't get enough of that warm, fresh blood.

My wife returned home late Thursday evening, and she apologized before wrapping my wounds and making me some chicken noodle soup and tucking me tightly into bed. She said that she didn't know what had come over her, but she was not all that believable. My wife had to feed the soup to me, as if I were a helpless little baby. I don't like her anymore.

Friday

Just when you think you know someone, they give you the biggest surprise of your life.

Jane was lying at the foot of my bed purring softly when I came to at about 6:25 AM. The sheets and covers were tucked so tightly around the remaining stump of my body that droplets of sweat covered my forehead, as if I had been lying on the sidewalk during a mild rainstorm. I screamed my wife's name, but I knew deep in my bones that she was gone forever.

With some rigorous shuffling and twitching, I wiggled myself loose from my wife's death cocoon. There was a handwritten note lying on her pillow.

The note had been written in red ink on one of those cheap notepads left by the neighborhood real estate agent. Realtor Chuck Flasher's photo beamed at me from the top left corner of the page. Chuck was wearing a toupee that was so cheap that I could see the seam clinging to dear life upon his aging forehead. But I had to give Chuck credit for having such courage. The man refused to change his last name despite all of the inevitable teasing, joking, and harassment throughout grades K-12, and far beyond, I'm sure. Not only did Chuck refuse to change his name, but he plastered it on notepads and spread them all over town, as a grown adult. I decided that I had to meet Chuck Flasher someday.

My wife's note started with the following: *I AM LEAVING YOU, DAN.* Well, at least she didn't beat around the bush. *I KNOW THAT WHAT I DID TO YOU WAS UNORTHODOX, BUT I WAS JUST TRYING TO KEEP YOU IN CHECK. I HAVE TRIED AND TRIED, BUT I JUST CAN'T TAKE IT ANYMORE — THE LATE NIGHTS WITH YOU COMING HOME REEKING OF BOOZE AND CHEAP WHORES FROM THE STRIP CLUB, YOUR PHILANDERING WITH THAT HUSSY JUDY FROM DOWN THE STREET AND YOUR SHAMELESS FLIRTING WITH THE SOCCER MOMS. YOU'RE LUCKY I LET YOU KEEP YOUR PECKER. ALSO, YOU SPEND MONEY LIKE A COMPLETE IDIOT, DAN, STARTING WITH YOUR $60,000 TRUCK AND THAT TACKY GOLD ROLEX YOU BOUGHT YOURSELF WITH THE KIDS' COLLEGE*

SAVINGS. WHO DO YOU THINK YOU ARE? TOM CRUISE CIRCA 1988? UNFORTUNATELY, YOU WILL ALWAYS BE THE SAME OLD PRICK THAT I MARRIED. AND WHAT'S WITH THE DISGUSTING MENTHOL CIGARETTES? THEY MAKE YOU SMELL LIKE A MINT CHIP ICE CREAM CONE DIPPED IN POO, BUT YOU DON'T SEEM TO CARE. PISSING ON THE TOILET SEAT, CONSTANTLY GRABBING MY ASS, WATCHING YOUR FAVORITE MOVIE, TAXI DRIVER, OVER AND OVER AGAIN (BY THE WAY, THAT'S A STUPID MOVIE — ITS JUST ABOUT A LONELY PSYCHOPATH DRIVING A TAXI CAB IN NEW YORK IN THE 1970'S), HOGGING THE COUCH, SNORING, BURPING, SLEEPING ALL AFTERNOON, IGNORING MY NEEDS, NOT LISTENING TO A WORD I SAY..."

She droned on and on with that letter, but I stopped reading after the first page. Maybe it's better this way. Old Jane and I make a pretty good pair, and we'll get this house whipped into shape in no time.

As I learned as a young chap, there are plenty of fish in the sea.

Winston Finds Oil

HIGH SCHOOL WAS COMING to an end and we were all scared to death. As we drank our beers and thought about the waves we had caught that day, we collectively gazed out over the mighty blue Pacific Ocean lying meekly beneath the all-powerful sun and pretended that we were somehow unaffected by the weight of it all.

1959 might seem like ancient history to you youngsters, but believe me, it isn't. It might as well have been last week. Put down your phones and pull up a chair and I'll tell you all about it.

Before the 1960s, Tucker Hill was just a sleepy little California town on the outskirts of Long Beach. There was nothing out there but a few cottages and shacks, with some stray coyotes roaming the hills.

And there was oil. In fact, there was so much oil that it would seep right through the ground in some places. A few of the small time oil men had been drilling around Tucker Hill since before the Depression and there were a few oil derricks scattered up and down the California coast. But the big oil companies had yet to invest the big bucks needed to suck all of that luscious black gold out of those virgin hills.

I ran with a pretty rowdy gang of kids back then. We were a little on the rambunctious side, but we all managed to stay out of jail. Except for Ronnie. A few years after high school, Ronnie wound up in prison for running a pyramid scheme. He told me he had needed the money because he was going through a divorce, but I had told him that the whole scam sounded like a loser from the outset. I suppose nothing makes a man more desperate for money than a divorce. Take my unsolicited advice, kids — sometimes it's cheaper to keep 'er , if you catch my drift.

Anyway, our gang spent the spring and summer months of high school surfing down at Seal Beach. You could say we were a bit on the lazy side. None of us could ever manage to wake up early enough to surf before dawn, so we would paddle out at Sunset Beach in the late afternoon after the wind calmed down and the water turned smooth and glassy.

After surfing, we would stop by the liquor store and grab whatever beer we could get ours hands on. Howard was the only one in our crew who was twenty-one, so we would all pitch in a few bucks and send him into Winner's Circle Liquor to pick up a case of Lucky Lager. Howard would always refuse to chip in for the beer because he said he deserved payment for his "services." He always was a cheap bastard and none of us bothered fighting with him about it.

Back then, the boards were so big and heavy that there

were only a few ways to haul them down to the beach. That
year I had bought an old black hearse at an auction for two
hundred dollars, which made me the official "surf chauffeur"
for the summer.

After securing the Lucky Lager from the liquor store, I
would drive the hearse up a narrow dirt trail to the top of
Tucker Hill. The guys sat in the back of the hearse with the
boards, while Fred rode shotgun with me up front. We would
hang out at the top of the hill, drinking one Lucky Lager after
another, while watching the sun set over the dark blue Pacific
Ocean.

Scattered across the smaller hills just below us, we spied
dozens of men from the oil company. They had already built a
handful of oil derricks on Tucker Hill, but they still had a lot of
work to do. It was obvious that the lion's share of oil had yet to
be yanked from the ground, as the men worked in shifts
around the clock. Just as the sun set and the sky grew violently
dark, floodlights would flip on and cast a blinding glare from
one hill to the next. The men never stopped working and
searching.

Actually, the men themselves did not do much searching.
One day I heard a low, deep howling. ARRROOOOOOOH!! Then I
saw a little pooch sniffing and strutting all over those hills. He
was a brown and white basset hound with just about the
longest, floppiest ears I'd ever seen. This dog moved like a big
husky clown and he was born to do just one thing: sniff. Boy,

could that dog sniff up a storm. Up, down, and all over Tucker Hill.

At first, we couldn't tell what that old basset hound was searching for. He would scour the hills and a cluster of men from the oil company would follow close behind. Sometimes, the basset hound would wander off deep into the bushes, and the oil men would yell, "Winston, get on back here now!"

Winston would sniff and trot his way all up and down those hills, past the oil derricks and through the bushes, all day long and into the night. It eventually occurred to me that the oil men had Winston out there sniffing for black gold from down below.

Apparently, Winston's nose was so damn strong that he could tell where the pockets of oil were lying underneath the soil.

If Winston sniffed over a hill or two and he didn't smell any oil, he would look back at the men and shake his head back and forth as if to say, *"NO OIL HERE, BOYS."*

Once the oil men got that signal from Winston, they would make their way over to the work trucks and the whole crew would get to work setting up tents in those oil free zones. Since the oil men had to live on the work site, they needed to pitch their tents on a spot where they wouldn't have to worry about oil exploding up out of the ground and shooting them into the air like a dirty black lava volcano.

But let me tell you, once Winston caught himself a whiff of some of that precious black gold with his wet nostrils, he put on quite a show. The first thing Winston would do was stick out his left paw as straight as a flag pole. It was always the left paw, for some reason. Then Winston would take that left paw and draw a great big X in the dirt. But Winston couldn't stop himself there, because I guess he couldn't contain his own excitement. He would do this little dance in front of the X. His rump and tail would sway side to side like an old lady dancing in a conga line at a wedding. Then for the big finale, Winston would stick his snout straight up into the air with his floppy ears dangling in the wind and make a terrific deep howl. *AARRROOOOOOH!*

I suppose that's how a basset hound says, *"PUT THE PEDAL TO THE METAL BOYS, WE'VE GOT SOME OIL HERE!"*

That's all it took for the oil men to start building an oil derrick, night and day. There was no telling how little time they had before that black lava started shooting right out of the ground, and those stingy oil bastards didn't want to miss out on one single dime of profit. You've never seen an oil crew work so fast. It seemed like those wooden planks appeared out of nowhere and an army of shirtless men would hammer so fast and hard it sounded like the world's most obnoxiously loud typewriter running at about two-hundred and fifty words a minute.

Those oil men had a good thing going with Winston. He

was a loyal old pooch who was always more than happy to help those men find oil. But even the most loyal of dogs have their limits, and those oil men never gave Winston a single minute of rest.

One evening at dusk I was sitting on top of the hill with Fred throwing back a few Lucky Lagers, and I'll be damned if they didn't have poor Winston running at full speed from one hill to the next, sniffing through bushes, trees, and cacti. At one point Winston stuck out his tongue and I could see his ribs heaving in and out like a bony old steam engine just about ready to shoot out one last puff of steam before dying. But those men kept dragging Winston up one hill and down the next like he was some sort of mechanical mule.

Once the sun finally passed down behind the hills to take a rest for the evening, Winston was allowed to curl up on an old dirty blanket, where one of the men would throw him a spoonful of mush and a tiny bowl of water. Winston was so exhausted that he barely touched the mush, and took just a few licks of water.

Here's where things get interesting. About a week later a real nice swell brought us some good waves and I was surfing with the gang at Sunset Beach all afternoon. I drove the hearse back up to our usual spot on the hill before sundown, and there we were drinking beer and smoking Pall Malls and jawboning about a bunch of nothing. Howard unveiled his great big plan to join the Navy, but Artie broke the news to him that he would probably spend four years washing dishes and cleaning toilets instead of commanding a fleet of battleships in the South Pacific.

About two hundred feet down the hill we saw poor old Winston making his rounds, looking for new oil spots. I couldn't help but notice that Winston looked like he had had all of the fight kicked out of him. His snout was almost scraping the dirt, his tail was dragging, and he had a slight limp at his front left paw. Maybe some of the oil men got drunk and beat Winston when his snout failed to find the goods. Maybe Winston had come down with a nasty case of the doggy flu. Perhaps Winston was just tired. After all these years, I still can't figure out what happened with Winston, but what I saw that day made me realize that those who roam the earth on four paws understand more than we realize.

Winston sniff sniff sniffed his way up and down the hill. At one point, he stopped and stuck out his left paw, looking like he was ready to draw a big giant X in the dirt and begin his little doggy dance to show that he found oil. It looked like his paws were getting stuck in something gooey in the dirt, and I could see him struggling to take small steps. Then suddenly, Winston put his left paw down, and just kept walking.

He looked back at the men and slowly shook his head. *"NO OIL HERE, BOYS."*

Winston went back to camp and curled up on his dirty old blanket, allowing himself just a few sips of water but skipping dinner altogether.

Just before sundown, the oil fellas set up a whole row of tents where Winston had been sniffing that afternoon. As the men settled down in their tents and made a campfire, Winston curled up on his dirty old blanket and gazed upon the crew with his dirty old brown eyes. It appeared as if Winston was sleeping, but he was watching intently. Watching and waiting. Breathing and sighing. Down in the newly made camp, Winston could hear cups clinking, bottles clanking, and drunken men hollering.

Winston licked his lips, and his muzzle formed a little doggy smile.

The ground rumbled ever so slightly, as if baby demons in hell were having a slumber party and were passing around a stolen bottle of daddy's Jack Daniels. The sound of the rumbling stayed constant, but the intensity continued to grow. One of the men in the camp sat upon an old log and stomped both feet squarely on the ground and was as still as a bronze statue, as his ass rumbled beneath him.

"What in the hell is that?" he asked the others.

Before one of the other dirty faced men had a chance to respond, the earth opened beneath them and a filthy, greasy, black ocean blasted every one of them straight into the atmosphere. Tent poles, chairs, wooden stumps, and sleeping bags exploded upward like the dirtiest and blackest Fourth of July fireworks show you'd ever seen.

Winston instantaneously perked up, lifted his left paw and pointed it at the cluster of horrified, oil covered men below him. He wiggled his rump and shook his tail with a kind of zest and ecstasy I had never seen any other living creature exhibit. And then Winston's outrageous howl smothered all the land.

AARRROOOOOH!!!

Winston gathered his composure, straightened his spine, and casually and regally trotted down Tucker Hill and headed straight toward the Pacific Ocean.

Four Doors

SAM TENTATIVELY WALKED up a few stairs to enter the living room and felt violently unwelcome as the fragile wood creaked obnoxiously beneath the thick rubber soles of his Birkenstocks. The brown wooden stairs had a nice cosmetic appearance, but they were flimsy because the sellers of this house were frugal bastards. Actually, not just frugal. The sellers were cheap, stingy sons of bitches who would squeeze Sam and his young family for every penny they had ever earned.

Despite the subpar stairs, the entrance to the craftsman style house was quite charming. A red door with a brass knocker. Not an obnoxious American Beauty kind of red, but a respectable, suburban, Republican red. The type of door that will let passersby know that hard-working and responsible people sleep in this house on warm summer nights. The respectably red door with the brass knocker opened into a great room full of ostentatiously high windows and unforgiving sunlight. Sam noticed his "transitions" eyeglasses turning a darkish yellow, as he hung a left and made his way into the bright white kitchen.

Certainly a family had lived here, but the house had been

staged by professionals to squeeze every last drop of blood out of the unsuspecting purchasers. Sam had a hard time deciding what the staging professionals were trying to accomplish with their curious decorating decisions. Surely they were trying to create a sense of warmth, safety, security, and prosperity. What they had done, however, was turn a nice family house into the illusion of a home inhabited by accomplished but boring individuals.

The kitchen counters were completely empty. Not a cup, spoon, cutting board, towel, or utensil in sight. The family room made Sam chuckle out loud. Two small love seats faced each other, directly adjacent to a wood-burning fireplace. No TV, and no place for a TV anywhere downstairs. Every wall consisted of floor-to-ceiling windows, with the exception of the big, stupid fireplace. No place for a recliner to read books at night, and no place to lie down and take an afternoon nap. This was a house built for a couple of chatty Cathys who want to sit by the fireplace all night long in the smoldering Southern California heat and jawbone the night away. *WHO WANTS TO LIVE IN AN UNCOMFORTABLE HOUSE LIKE THIS?*

"Oh my God, this family room is absolutely adorable. It's so cozy and cute. The natural light in the kitchen is just what we've been looking for, right honey," said Sam's wife, Nancy. *WOMEN DON'T CHAT, THEY CONSPIRE.*

Beads of hot salty sweat formed on Sam's upper lip, as he turned towards Nancy and managed a half grin out of the left corner of his mouth.

"I'm going to take a look upstairs," said Sam, motioning toward the realtor.

"You go right ahead," said the realtor, with an approving nod, as if Sam had needed her permission.

Sam regretted hiring a woman realtor. He could already hear the two of them chatting and cackling down below in the kitchen, and of course the realtor would give Nancy the hard sale to buy this torture rack of a house, a place where Sam would never have a chance to enjoy a Rams game on Sunday or recline in his chair at night and read his true crime books. *I SWEAR, THEY'RE ALL IN IT TOGETHER.*

The top of the stairs opened up into a long hallway, breaking to the left at a sharp angle. The hallway was long and dark and was covered with carpet that was short and tightly wound. The carpet was brand new and was bordered by thick, white crown molding. The hallways were freshly painted light gray. A skylight in the middle of the hallway produced some ambient light, but a heavy darkness engulfed the small amount of light that made its way through, smothering it with the obsessive embrace of a murderous mother.

Four bedroom doors emanated from the hallway, with each one permitting just a trickle of sunlight to spill onto the light brown hallway carpet. Sam stood there for a moment, stiff like a Swiss guard at the Vatican, with his arms at his side and his palms turned inward toward his thighs. The high-pitched voices of Nancy and the realtor slowly faded away, as if a brittle winter's wind was delicately blowing them to the other side of the universe. Sam continued to sweat, as heat generated from the floor and made its way up through his Birkenstocks and into his feet and calves. Sam stood there, basking in the increasing silence and enjoying the soothing heat.

Straight ahead and to the right, Sam heard the hinges of the door from the first bedroom creak, as the door slowly opened, causing the patch of light in the hallway to flourish. Sam was overtaken by an all consuming sense of peace and well being. *THIS IS WHAT IT MUST FEEL LIKE TO SHOOT HEROIN.*

Sam slipped off his Birkenstocks and placed them at the far corner of the hallway. His bare feet felt welcome and comfy on the soft brown carpet. He spread his toes outward, then scrunched them inward, hearing each individual metatarsal crack and pop itself into place. By the time Sam had taken his first few steps down the hallway, his head felt warm and fuzzy and tingly. Sam turned and looked back over his shoulder for Nancy and the realtor, but the house was dead silent. They were both gone. Maybe not physically gone, but as far as Sam was concerned, neither of them existed anymore.

Sam found himself inside the first bedroom sooner than he had expected. He stood in the center of the room with his bare feet spread wide and his hands at his hips, as if he were about to embark on some great adventure. The room was empty and the walls were painted bright white — the kind of white paint that is used when trashy apartments are being prepped and cleaned after nightmare tenants have spent the past six months gulping from beer bongs and blasting old Motley Crue songs until 4 AM. *NOTHING TO SEE HERE.*

Sam gently closed the door to the first room, and made his way down the hallway. He placed his hand on the doorknob of the second door, but the knob felt cold and uninteresting. Without twisting the door knob, Sam let go, and walked farther down the hallway.

Sam arrived at the third door, which was just slightly ajar. As he peaked his head as close as possible to the crack in the door, he heard a tremendous howling sound, as if a terrible room tornado were creating itself in its own image in the center of the empty room. Sam took a quick step back and slammed the door shut, setting his sights upon the end of the hallway.

A small, handwritten sign had been taped to the dead center of the door of the fourth room. The writing was too small for Sam to read at that distance, so he took a few steps forward. The handwriting was sloppy and childish. *LOOK IN HERE,* it said.

Before he realized what was happening, Sam's trembling, sweaty right palm had gripped itself around the door knob at the end of the hallway. Sam's right arm whipped the door open so hard that a gust of wind blasted back into his face, rustling his hair and moving his eyelashes just a tad.

The inside of the fourth room was dark and there was a

single light bulb hanging from a string in the center of the ceiling, casting a harsh shadow upon each and every object. The wind from Sam's dramatic entrance had caused the light bulb to sway back and forth, making the shadows perform a sly dance along the walls, rocking too and fro. A mysterious tugboat finding its way along the deep blue sea.

A dark navy blue cloth chair occupied the far left corner of the empty room. A hand written sign safety-pinned to the arm of the chair read: SIT DOWN HERE. Sam removed the sign, held it in his hands, and studied it with an imbecile's curiosity. Sam then sat down as instructed. The chair was comfortable and warm, but not in an inviting way. Something truly awful had happened here.

The absolute silence within the fourth room made Sam's ears ring, which made his heart beat rapidly, which in turn made his brow sweat profusely. He was listening ever so hard, without hearing a thing.

The door opened and a colorful presence entered the room, placing itself squarely between Sam and the door. Sam thought he could see a hodgepodge of rainbow colors, but he was not sure. He could definitely feel it, though. Something between shock, fright, giddiness, and unfiltered horror. Whatever it was, it was wholeheartedly interested in Sam and wanted something from him real bad.

Sam had given up on trying to see this thing, whatever it was, so he lied on his stomach and placed his ear directly onto the hardwood floor, hearing and feeling hysterical laughter mixed with guttural crying and primitive screaming. *COME WITH US. WE'LL MAKE A NICE PLACE FOR YOU.*

Sam rose to his knees and straightened his back, and stuck out both of his hands with his palms facing toward the ceiling. The laughing and screaming and crying became louder and louder until Sam's skull was filled with a cornucopia of bouncing ghosts. His inner being felt warm and at peace for the first time since he was a little boy. *I WILL GO WITH YOU NOW.*

A great wind swept the room, flinging the blue cloth chair through the window and down onto the dead brown lawn in the backyard. The wind was so intense that Sam could not open his eyes, and he felt as if his eardrums would rupture at any moment. The great warmth within his core strengthened, until Sam realized that he was already gone from the house and his wife and the realtor, realizing the life he had known was gone forever.

Midnight Pier

IT STARTED OFF as a drunken dare. There was a girl involved, too. A rather pretty girl, in fact. The girl had been making bedroom eyes at Cameron from the other end of the bar all night. The more the girl looked at him, the more Cameron would drink, to make it appear as if he had some urgent business that required his attention. But Cameron couldn't blame the girl, if he were being honest, because he had agreed to jump from Balboa pier on his own accord.

Somehow Cameron and his pals had ended up drinking shots of "Three Wise Men" — some sort of whiskey concoction his buddy Tom had been championing all night. Cameron wasn't sure how many shots he had let fly down his gullet, but before he knew it, he and Tom and the rest of the boys were slugging each other in the shoulders and lying about which girls they had felt up in high school. Cameron couldn't tell who exactly was hitting him, but his lips had gone numb and he no longer noticed the hard fists smashing into his biceps.

Later in the evening, there were vague grumblings and then an argument about how cold the ocean water was in January, and how high the top of Balboa pier was from the ocean surface at high tide. Then someone pulled out their phone and confirmed that high tide would be at midnight, right on the button!

Not long after, there was a sloppy walk along the wooden planks of the pier, with Cameron's rubbery legs leading the charge. All of the boys walked together, like a drunken swarm of noisy, lost bees.

Somehow Cameron had volunteered for the task, or perhaps someone had elected him in mental absentia. Either way, Cameron had managed to crawl over the low wooden railing at the edge of the pier. He stood as erect as British royalty, with the white rubber tips of his Converse confidently pointing straight and true toward the center of the Pacific Ocean.

The moon was full and the water was black. The ocean mist felt like soft wet kisses from the goddess of Atlantis. Cameron felt the wind rushing against his face and ruffling his hair into a terrible mess. His stomach suddenly and without apologies rushed up into his sternum, as if there were an elevator running straight up his core. Cameron had no recollection of jumping from the pier, but when he looked down, a black sheet of water was racing toward his frightened feet so fast that he never even had time to scream.

Cameron hadn't imagined that he would hit the water so hard, or that he would sink so deep. But what surprised him the most was the intensity of nature's merciless cold. The water did not surround his body as much as it attacked him with unexplained hostility.

The Three Wise Men were in his belly and they watched over him, though, keeping his skin warm, his muscles loose, and his mind calm. Cameron looked toward shore and the city lights didn't look so far away. *ONE STROKE AT A TIME, AND I'LL BE BACK ON THE SAND BEFORE I KNOW IT.*

It wasn't long before he felt it. Not so much a nudge or a pull, but instead it felt as if the pressure of the entire universe had attached itself to his left calf. The twisting and the shaking soon followed, and even a drunken Cameron knew there could only be one explanation. *FISHERMEN HAVE BEEN SPOTTING GREAT WHITES FROM THE PIER ALL WINTER.*

Cameron reached down and grabbed hold of the nose of the sea beast, which felt like sandpaper that had been lying in the Mojave desert all summer long. The nose ripped away from Cameron's hand, only to resume its shaking and nodding. Cameron reached out again, far past the nose, feeling a gelatinous orb at the side of the head of the beast. He pressed with his thumb harder and harder, until he felt a pop, followed by a sensation that his thumb had broken through a water balloon full of vegetable oil. But the one eyed shark kept going, as if it had been training for this moment its whole life. *I GUESS THIS IS IT, THEN.*

Without warning, Cameron heard the roar of the water from his right side and under the full moon, a glistening dorsal fin about the size of an American flag came racing toward the sea beast attached to his leg. Faster than a greased up naked mole rat shooting down a water slide, the great white barreled toward Cameron with its jaws wide open, exposing nature's most cruel and diabolical weapon. The great white didn't seem to notice Cameron, as it soared right past him, sinking its teeth into the sea beast attached to Cameron's leg. *OH MY GOD, THEY'RE CANNIBALS!*

The sea beast released Cameron's calf, as if a sharky dentist had told it to open wide. Cameron splashed and kicked the water, to create distance between himself and these two magnificent gladiators of the sea. He watched in awe for a few seconds, as the newcomer great white devoured the sea beast without any tremendous effort. The champion great white, having finished off its foe, slowly circled around Cameron a few times, before the American flag dorsal fin confidently sunk itself back into the sea like a World War II submarine.

One stroke at a time, Cameron made his way to shore. He wanted to just lie on the wet sand for awhile, and take it all in. His buddies approached and circled around him, and no one said a word. Tom stared at Cameron slack-jawed, with his arms hanging at his side, a matching set of wet noodles. Tom took off his belt and cinched it around Cameron's leg to stop the bleeding.

"It was just a goof, man. We didn't think you would really jump from the pier."

Cameron looked up at the sky, appreciating the brightness of the stars and planets, wondering if anyone out there in the universe might be staring back at him through a telescope. He gazed at Tom, managing to produce a pathetic grin and a drunken wink.

"It's all right man, the Three Wise Men were with me the whole way."

Scuffle at Wet Mule Bank

ZEKE KNEW SOMETHING wasn't right by the way the bank teller stood at stiff attention, with a curious smile splattered across his face.

For three years, Zeke had trusted that all of his money had been secure at Wet Mule Bank in the town of Cold Shadow, Arizona territory. He had become quite accustomed to a casual wave and a friendly greeting from the teller, Bartholomew, each and every Friday when he strolled in to make his deposit after a rough week at the lumber mill.

Zeke took a peak behind the counter and spied a small mirror hanging on the wall behind the teller. He supposed the gals at the bank made use of the mirror to doll themselves up before quitting time.

But there was a sudden flash in the mirror, about as quick as a lightning bug getting gobbled up by a hungry frog on a lilly pad. Zeke stared closer into the mirror, and saw a side profile of a man wearing a black trench coat and a black hat, wielding a shiny hunting knife. The man stood just to the right of Bartholomew. That hunting knife had caught the sun's rays in such a way that it shot punishing beams first into the mirror, then into Zeke's eyes. Zeke looked at Bartholomew with a look of pure solemnity.

"I'll be gosh darned, Bartholomew, but I left the satchel with my money at Aristocrat Saloon. I'll be right back," said Zeke, lifting his hat off his head while scratching his balding scalp with his middle finger.

Bartholomew's face was flush, and a hot stream of dirty sweat made its trek from the corner of his eye down to his shaky chin.

Zeke did his darnedest to appear casual as he hustled himself out of Wet Mule Bank. His horse, Darla, was waiting for him out front. Zeke slid his boot into the stirrup and whipped himself up into the hard leather saddle.

"Come on old girl, let's take a ride," said Zeke to Darla.

Darla slowly walked around to the back of Wet Mule Bank, dutifully coming to a halt at the rear door. Zeke hopped down, patted Darla affectionately on the neck, and looked into her understanding eyes.

"You just sit tight until I need you, old girl. I've got to go take care of some business and help my old friend Bartholomew."

The back door to Wet Mule Bank opened quietly when Zeke placed his fingers on the boards and pressed just a little. Zeke heard some faint whimpers emanating from the back room, next to the safe. He stealthily glided toward the safe, one step at a time, walking on tiptoes in his brown cowhide boots. With each step, the whimpering grew louder and louder, until

Zeke spied two of the teller girls sitting on the floor with their wrists tied behind their backs. Their feet were tied up too, and bandannas had been secured around their heads and stuffed into their mouths. Desperate tears streamed down the face of the busty redhead closest to Zeke.

Zeke got good and close to the girls, squatted down in front of them, then placed his finger over his lips. *Shhhh!*

The weight of Zeke's Colt 45 Peacemaker felt comforting against his left hip. Zeke reached to his right side, placing his palm squarely around the handle of his knife. Although Zeke wanted to pull out his Peacemaker and go to work, he knew that silence would help him win the day. He drew the knife from its sheath, admiring the long heartlessness of the shiny blade. He held the blade out before him, as it guided him toward the teller window. Zeke's moves were more quiet than a rattlesnake on a hot prairie night.

And there he stood. The bandit was dressed in black, with a red bandanna tied around his face, covering his nose and mouth. Bartholomew was tied up in the corner, and as soon as he saw Zeke, his eyes turned bigger than twin full moons on the summer solstice. Zeke looked at Bartholomew and shook his head. *Shhhh!*

The bandit was bent over in the corner, stuffing bundles of money into a black suede bag. Zeke just stood there for a moment, more frozen than a Montana morning in January.

Then Zeke sprung at the bandit. He swiped the knife at the

bandit's back, but the bandit had sensed him coming and slithered out of the way just in time. The knife wiggled out of Zeke's hand and slid across the dusty wooden floor like a crooked stone skipping across an arid creek bed.

Zeke leaped through the air, straight toward the bandit, more graceful than a flying squirrel. The bandit grunted, as Zeke's chest slapped down onto the bandit's hefty back. The bandit collapsed into the floor boards, as if a collection of sandbags had fallen from the ceiling. Zeke's right arm whipped itself around the bandit's neck, providing Zeke a firm and confident hold. Zeke's face turned red and blue veins popped out of his forehead, as he pull, pull, pulled, with his bicep, crushing one side of the neck, and his meaty forearm squeezing the other side. The bandit's boots kicked wildly, scuffing and clawing at the floorboards. In less than 10 seconds, the bandit's body went lifeless and limp.

He's not dead, just out cold.

* * *

The bandit woke up shivering, with his skin painfully tight and his ears encrusted with dirt, lying in the middle of the barren road in front of Wet Mule Bank. He was more naked than a seal pup in the snow. The town folk surrounded the bandit, with their cold and hard eyes shattering his broken soul into a million tiny pieces.

Zeke stepped up to the bandit, and threw him his pants, boots, and nothing more.

"Friend, you've got about 60 seconds to make your way out of town, before the ugly begins."

Darla slowly wandered up behind Zeke, snorting at the bandit, while shuffling her hoofs into the dirt in a way that made the bandit stop what he was doing and stare at the horse, slack-jawed and confused. A tall, thin woman wearing a white bonnet and a torn blue dress ran up from behind Darla and threw a rectangular dirt clod, which struck the bandit on his left temple, before exploding and cascading down over his shivering torso.

The bandit's chin started to tremble, and his eyes filled with clear water. He bent over and slipped on his boots, then crumpled his pants into a ball and placed them over his crotch. The bandit solemnly marched straight down the middle of the road and out of Cold Shadow, with his naked backside leaving the onlookers.

Darla stood behind Zeke, rubbing her nose gently against his head. Zeke patted Darla's snout, while watching the bandit disappear into the cloudy horizon.

"We did real good, old girl. Real good."

Into the Badlands

JEFFREY PRESSED HIS left index finger three times against the cracked and crusty button in the wall before he accepted that the doorbell was broken. Jeffrey then spied a brass door knocker, about 8 inches above the top of his head. Spider webs connected the knocker to the door, so Jeffrey used the tips of his fingers and thumb to quickly slam the hunk of brass against the door three times before any black widow could have a chance to sink it's filthy fangs into him.

A phlegmy cough pierced the air as the front door whipped open, causing a gust of wind and dead leaves to rush from the porch into the old house. Jeffrey fixed his eyes squarely upon an old, disheveled gentleman, well past his prime. White hair aggressively sprouted this way and that, as if tiny magical elves had planted "old man seeds" onto the man's scalp and earlobes in the middle of the night.

"Well, howdy do, kiddo. You sure are punctual, I'll give you that. It's 10 AM, right on the dot. I bet your ma and pa taught you the importance of being on time, now didn't they? I appreciate your resourcefulness, young fella. Not many kids these days have the get up and go to staple flyers around the neighborhood advertising yard work and handyman services. Anywho, come on in and get yourself situated. I've got plenty of work to keep you busy, if you've got the nerve, that is. Follow me upstairs."

An intense brightness assaulted Jeffrey as he made his way up the staircase, tailing the old man. A row of chandeliers with obnoxiously white light bulbs hung from the ceiling, and countless florescent lamps lined the walls. Jeffrey brought his right hand up to his eyebrow to shield his delicate eyes from it all.

"I like it nice and bright in here. Keeps the spooks away. Don't be shy kiddo, follow me," said the old man.

The old man's bony ass shifted from side to side with each step up the staircase, as his dirt-encrusted, brown leather work boots cautiously maneuvered up up up, one step at a time. Brown wool trousers were held together by tight red suspenders that looped up and over the old man's rotting shoulders. A beaten, short-sleeved, white-collared, office work shirt covered what was left of the old man's back and torso — the kind of shirt that engineers wear with a cheap polyester tie and a pocket protector. Black spots and freckles adorned the old man's wrinkled elbows, forearms, and hands.

Once at the top of the staircase, the old man stopped and stood rigid for a moment, as he appeared to be contemplating something incredibly important. He then came out of his trance and took short but deliberate steps to the right.

"Right this way, kiddo."

The hallway was covered with dirty brown shag carpet. A

narrow strip down the middle of the hallway was beaten and worn, while the edges of the carpet were thick and plush. The old man stopped in the hallway after five paces, placing both feet next to each other, as if he were standing at attention during Marine cadet training. The old man's head creaked up toward the ceiling, and Jeffrey's eyes followed. The ceiling was covered with popcorn acoustic insulation from the 1970s. A 4 foot x 2 foot hatch with a hanging rope handle caught Jeffrey's eye.

"Up there, kiddo. That's where you're going to earn your keep this afternoon. I call it The Badlands."

Jeffrey looked at the old man, then at the hatch that had been cut through the popcorn acoustic ceiling by construction workers singing along to Ted Nugent on the radio in 1977. Jeffrey had heard stories about sinister serial killers who lured unsuspecting teenagers into their homes. But this nutty old coot looked pretty harmless. Perhaps the old man wanted Jeffrey to rummage through storage trunks full of photo albums and unsalvageable camping gear.

"What kind of work do you need me to do up there in the attic — I mean, in The Badlands?"

The old man took a long and troubling stare at the hatch in the ceiling. He placed his thumb and index finger onto his eyeballs and rubbed with concerning vigor. If he rubbed any harder, Jeffrey was afraid the old man's eyeballs would burst and eyeball gel would squirt out of the old man's face.

"That's a bit hard to explain, kiddo. I've had a few other fellas come out here and try to handle The Badlands, but they all ended up running out of this house of mine with their tails tucked between their legs. I'll tell you what, if you can get the job done, this here is yours."

The old man retrieved a crisp $100 bill from his back pocket and held it up to the light in front of Jeffrey's face, as if the two of them were admiring a fancy work of art at the Louvre. Jeffrey nearly chuckled, but he stopped himself just in time once he realized that the old man was dead serious.

"I can't tell you no more than that, kiddo. Either you've got the stomach for this kind of work, or you don't. I would climb up there and tame The Badlands myself if I didn't have a bum ticker," said the old man, taking his right index finger and tapping it twice over his left pectoral.

"I just can't handle that type of stress no more. But you're young and full of piss and vinegar. So, you climb up there and clean up The Badlands for me, then you can slip old Benjamin Franklin here right into your back pocket and have yourself a grand night on the town with the young gal of your choosing. Hell, it shouldn't take no more than 20 minutes tops to finish the job."

Jeffrey gazed at the crisp hundred dollar bill floating in front of his nose. With that greenback in his pocket, Jeffrey could spend an entire weekend at the Retroplex movie theater by himself, watching one 70s flick after another while gorging on Junior Mints and buttered popcorn sprinkled with M&Ms. The Retroplex would be having a Martin Scorsese film festival this weekend, which was sure to delight. Hell, Jeffrey would even have enough dough left over to buy himself a fistful of Abba Zabbas and a triple scoop of mint and chip at Cecile's Ice Cream Metropolis on the corner of 5th and Main Street for at least three days in a row.

"You've got yourself a deal, old-timer. Hand me that there flashlight so I can get to work," said Jeffrey.

Jeffrey took a deep breath and placed his foot onto the ladder leading up to the attic, while gripping the side rails with his hands and holding the rubber flashlight with his teeth. An intense bright light emanated from the top of the stairwell leading into the attic, with obnoxious beams shooting themselves onto the top of Jeffrey's head. He noticed that his slow moving body parts were creating cartoonish but serious shadows along the ladder and the walls in the hallway. Jeffrey looked back and saw the old man peering up at him with curious and scared eyes and a crinkled brow that attempted to assure Jeffrey that he had made the right decision.

A low level hum surrounded Jeffrey's head as he entered the attic and stood upright. His eyes partially adjusted to the intense whiteness that possessed the room. The humming grew louder, until Jeffrey felt his cranium and eardrums vibrating uncomfortably.

"Look out for the boogies. They'll break you down if you

don't keep your guard up," said the old man.

"What in the hell is a boogie?" shouted Jeffrey.

"Don't you worry sonny boy, you'll know one when you see it. Those boogie bastards have been keeping me awake for months and I can't take it no more. I'm starting to lose my damn marbles. So you catch those boogie bastards and kill them dead so I can get some shut eye," hollered the old man.

Looking toward the air vent at the far end of the attic, Jeffrey noticed a brief flickering. A tiny speck of intense, white light grew into a massive orb that filled the attic with painful heat. The orb slowly opened in the middle, creating a hollow center before breaking into pieces and forming hundreds of tiny white skulls. The skulls poured from the air vent and shot in straight formation toward Jeffrey's face. He was unable to duck in time, and the skulls moved right through him. The deep humming became louder and more intense with each passing skull. Jeffrey felt his head vibrating, as if someone had jammed tiny back massagers into his ear canals. He swatted the flashlight toward the approaching skulls a few times, but it was no use. The skulls kept coming faster, the white light became brighter, and the deep humming became louder.

"Hey old-timer, why don't you come up here and give me a hand. I almost have these boogies under control, but I need you to hold the flashlight for me so I can get them corralled into one spot."

"No way, sonny boy. Like I told you, my bum ticker can't

handle that kind of excitement no more. You've got to handle this job yourself if you want to get old Benjamin Franklin here into your pocket."

"Sir, if you don't get up here and help me, I'm outta here."

The old man paced the hallway with his arms folded and his lips puckered. He hadn't slept in fourteen days and that's more than enough time for a man's mind to become his worst enemy. The old man scurried up the ladder and poked his head into the attic, scanning the room with terrified and exhausted eyes.

Jeffrey spotted the old man and motioned with his right hand for him to come closer, while he used his left hand to point the flashlight at the boogies.

"Here, you hold the flashlight on them, and I'll try to gather them into this one corner," said Jeffrey.

The old man took the flashlight from Jeffrey with a shaky hand and pointed it the best he could toward the cluster of white skulls. The white skulls had been floating about lazily, in no particular order, but when the old man approached and pointed the flashlight at them, each white skull became still and stared with great purpose at the old man. The old man's hand shook even worse, causing the light to bounce sporadically all over the wall.

"Hold the light steady, dammit. I need to see where to send the rest of them," shouted Jeffrey.

Jeffrey heard a thump, and whipped around to see that the

wall had been overcome by blackness. The old man was lying stiff as a board on his back, as the flashlight gracefully floated out of his hand and rolled across the attic floor. Jeffrey tried to pull at the old man's leg, but the old man felt frozen to the touch, even through his trousers. His body was as stiff as a tongue depressor and Jeffrey saw that his mouth was open in an O shape, with his jaw hanging down and back toward his Adam's apple. The sight reminded Jeffrey of the barbershop quartet on Main Street at Disneyland on hot summer days, and how their mouths would take a similar form when they would hold a baritone note longer than necessary.

The white skulls lined up in formation and hovered over the old man's body, close to his chest. For a long brief moment, the skulls sat there, calmly keeping vigil above the old man, getting one last look at him. Then one at a time the white skulls entered the old man's chest, causing his body to jerk violently with each encounter. The last skull wiggled its way through the old man's chest and his entire body lit up like a 1,000 watt light bulb. Jeffrey slapped his hand over his eyes and peeked through a narrow slit between his index finger and middle finger, and saw the old man's body rise from the attic floor and rotate like a slow moving ceiling fan, all the while glowing like a dirty chunk of nuclear waste.

The old man's body then dropped to the floor, and the crash was so loud that Jeffrey involuntarily slapped his hands over his ears and shrieked like a cranky infant. The lights had gone off and the old man's body was dark now, with rotten smoke rising from his face. Jeffrey knelt down on one knee and placed his fingers onto the old man's neck to check for a pulse. *So this is what death feels like.*

Jeffrey spied a gray and white knitted wool blanket in the corner of the attic. He affectionately set the blanket over the old man's uninhabited body, and retrieved the $100 bill from the old man's back pocket. This mission may or may not have been a technical success, but Jeffrey knew that he had earned his keep. More importantly, he knew that the old man would have wanted him to have the $100 bill.

The summer day was hot and merciless, and the air conditioning at the Retroplex Theater would cool Jeffrey's body and calm his mind. The Martin Scorsese Film Festival was starting at noon, and Jeffrey would finally have a chance to enjoy Taxi Driver in all its existential glory on the big screen.

Sarah Manor

"WATCH YOUR STEP, LADIES. Especially you gals there in the back with the high-heeled boots. There are plenty of boulders and holes out here, or 'ankle breakers,' as we like to call them. And Lord knows we don't need any lawsuits, so please take your time. Okay, how many of you are on your first trip to Napa Valley? Can you raise your hands? Wow! That's terrific! Well, it's my pleasure to welcome all of you to the breathtaking Sarah Manor. Built in 1899, this was the largest and most exquisite mansion and vineyard in all of Napa Valley at that time."

Bernie slowly waltzed his way up the hot and rocky dirt path lined with ancient, fat oak trees. The bark on the oak trees was so hard and unforgiving that it made Bernie wonder whether the oak trees liked being there at all.

Respectable khaki slacks smothered Bernie's legs, as a blue long sleeve shirt with a button-down collar stuck to his torso. A soft brown leather belt and even softer brown leather shoes with argyle beige and maroon socks made the preppy outfit complete. Stinky, smelly sweat covered Bernie from his neck line all the way down to his toe spaces. A row of water beads made themselves right at home atop Bernie's upper lip.

With his right hand tucked into a fist and jutted into the bottom of his ribs, Bernie's right elbow stuck out from his side like a stiff and pale rudder. Elizabeth's arm had clumsily looped its way through Bernie's right elbow. Her tan five inch heels managed to support her athletic frame, as a floral skirt hugged her hips and thighs so tightly that one innocent stumble would mean a broken wrist and a trip to the ER. Bernie could not help but feel at least partially ridiculous, as he and Elizabeth regally strutted up the dusty dirt path, as if they were the Duke and Duchess of Laguna Hills.

Bernie and Elizabeth were surrounded my many others who were masquerading through the arid, landlocked valley as if they were playing dress-up in one of those old West ghost towns where you can get your picture taken as the town sheriff or barkeep. Many of the women sported ostentatious hats with large and bright bows, with white gloves and Audrey Hepburn sunglasses. They would quietly chatter with friends, while taking in the sights and pointing toward beautiful landmarks. An unsuspecting tourist might figure these women had flocked to Napa Valley to learn about culture and appreciate wine making, but Bernie suspected they had come to get drunk and gossip.

"Oh I almost forgot, my name is Daphne. I'll be your tour guide today. I've got some great wine for all of you, so just follow me into the dining room and we'll get started.

Everything you see here was custom-built by Mordecai Nelson. Mordecai and his lovely wife Sarah lived here from 1899 until 1923. Their marriage was the stuff of legends. Books have been written about them! Mordecai loved Sarah sooooo much that he just kept building and building whatever she desired. If you look through this window you can see the first swimming pool in California — it was built right here! The lovely Sarah would run outside on scorching hot summer days and enjoy a cool dip in the water whenever she pleased. Sometimes I just gaze off into the valley and my heart melts when I think about all the fun Mordecai and Sarah must've had frolicking around this wine country paradise. They had a real passion for wine and a special love for one another, and this vineyard's continuing success is a testament to the love and passion of two truly amazing people."

Bernie did his best to follow along with Daphne's preamble, but his punishing hangover from the night before would not give him a pardon. He looked to his right and saw Elizabeth standing at attention with her gaze focused upon the enthusiastic Daphne. Elizabeth's pale chin was trembling ever so slightly, and Bernie spied a short parade of tears trickling from the far corners of her eyes. Elizabeth peered over towards Bernie with a look of pure love and tenderness in her eyes, the kind of look women reserve for newborn babies and weddings. Bernie did his best to respond with the type of half smile that would at least suggest that he was making an effort to sincerely enjoy himself.

"All right everybody, were going to start off with some reds. Grab a glass, and I'll be coming around with a lovely, rich Merlot blend," said Daphne.

Daphne pleasantly surprised Bernie by giving him a generous pour. Perhaps she had accurately pegged Bernie as a grumpy old prick who needed a stiff drink before he could enjoy a good time with his wife. Bernie splashed that Merlot down his gullet like a raging alcoholic who had just escaped a Mormon compound in Utah.

"A bit thirsty, are we," said Daphne with a tight lipped grin.

She gave him an even bigger pour, before making a graceful half spin on her high heels, to serve the others.

"All of the photos on the wall are of Mordecai and Sarah. I just love this one over here of the two of them standing at the front door. This photo was taken just after the construction had been completed. You can tell they were completely infatuated by each other, by their gazes. It's in the eyes! This is a great shot too — Mordecai and Sarah with their 11 children. They're still hugging each other, arm in arm, after all that time! Soooo much in love!"

The wine had finally done what it's job, and Bernie felt himself floating, a monarch butterfly caught in a gentle summer night's breeze.

"I have to use the little boy's room," said Bernie.

"It's upstairs. Hurry back before you miss the rest of the

tour," said Elizabeth, as she remained focused on Daphne, with her back facing Bernie.

* * *

Bernie expected the wooden stairs to be old and creaky, but in fact they were unforgiving and firm beneath the soles of his shoes. The staircase became darker and darker with each step upward, and when he finally reached the hallway at the top of the staircase, Bernie was standing in almost complete blackness, with his hand resting palm down on the railing. The pressure had been building in his lower abdomen for some time, and his bladder felt as if it were carrying thousands of sharp, tiny pine needles encased within a sea of hot urine.

Bernie burst through the first door at his right side, which luckily happened to be the bathroom. He managed to unzip his khaki pants and flop out his weiner with no more than a 10th of a second to spare before an angry, hot stream of clear urine shot into the toilet. The urine made a deep and hollow sound in the bowl that made Bernie feel as if he were actually accomplishing something magnificent. *ENLARGED PROSTATE. GODDAMN IT, I'M ONLY 50 YEARS OLD!*

The bathroom had a small dish next to the sink, containing tiny bars of soap in multiple colors, shaped like seashells. Bernie found that the tiny seashell soaps made him enjoy washing his hands much more than usual. Bernie finished in the bathroom by wiping his dripping wet hands onto a blue hand towel, before flipping the light switch down and returning to the hallway. *I MIGHT AS WELL TAKE A QUICK LOOK AROUND WHILE I'M UP HERE. IF ELIZABETH DOESN'T LIKE THAT I'M LOLLYGAGGING, I DON'T GIVE A SHIT.*

There were many doors lining the hallway, but the door at the end of the hallway seemed the most interesting. Bernie took a few tentative steps toward the door at the end of the hallway, but before he knew it, he was walking so quickly that his arms were flinging back and forth like a middle-aged women walking fast in the park for exercise because she can't run anymore.

Before he knew it, Bernie was at the end of the hallway, when his feet halted abruptly. When he reached his hand out to grip the door handle, he noticed just how slow and deliberate his arm and hand were moving. The door handle was made of glass and felt cold and unloving in the palm of Bernie's hand. As soon as Bernie's fingers wrapped around the door handle, it began to slowly shift back and forth within the palm of his hand. With each drawn out turn to the left and then to the right, the doorknob creaked a lonely series of notes, as if it were trying to tell Bernie something. The glass doorknob became hot in Bernie's hand, as the plain white door slowly swung wide. Bernie took a step forward, stood under the doorway, then made another step into the unfamiliar room.

The inside of the room was bright and hot and empty. All of the windows were closed, and the air was suffocating. A couple of fuzzy figures moved with the slow grace of ballerinas at the far end of the room by an un-curtained window, before coming into focus. THAT'S SARAH AND MORDECAI.

Mordecai approached Sarah with a slow but deliberate curiosity, as Sarah turned her back to him. Sarah's silky black hair ran the length of her back, coming to a conclusion just an inch past her hips. Mordecai gently placed his right hand onto Sarah's right shoulder and rubbed meekly. He leaned closer toward her and whispered something into her ear. Bernie saw the fuzzy outline of Mordecai's lips moving, as if he were watching an old black-and-white horror movie on a UHF channel in the game room of his childhood home. *ELVIRA'S MIDNIGHT HORROR BALL.*

Sarah's shoulders slumped forward and her head dropped, as if she were a narcolepsy patient having an episode. Sarah turned to face Mordecai, and they just stood there, nose to nose, in complete silence. They gazed into each other's eyes, and Bernie noticed the left corner of Mordecai's mouth turn upward in a tepid smile. Bernie stood there watching, realizing that he had not taken a sufficient breath for quite some time. He breathed in a hefty gulp of air, forcing his diaphragm to stick out. He held it there for a few seconds, then exhaled with precision.

Sarah moved her right hand upward and placed it onto Mordecai's forehead, lovingly caressing his hairline. This made Bernie's heart feel soft and warm. But when Bernie looked into

Sarah's eyes, he noticed they were hard and steely, as if she had been staring at a crossword puzzle for too long without thinking of the right word.

Sarah's right hand cunningly grabbed a thick chunk of Mordecai's bushy hair and yanked him brutally to his left side, causing him to collapse onto the hardwood floor with a THUD! Sarah had large feet for such a thin woman, and the flat bottom of her brown leather boot found its way onto Mordecai's Adam's apple. Sarah's boot gradually pressed harder and harder, as Mordecai's hands gripped themselves desperately around her ankle and calf. Mordecai's feet shot out from beneath him before the sharp edges of his boot heels whacked themselves into the floorboards, over and over again.

Bernie stood there stunned, with his arms rigidly pressed against his sides, as if he were stumbling through his first day on the job as a guard at Buckingham Palace. Sarah's face slowly turned its gaze away from Mordecai's impending doom, as she made fierce eye contact with Bernie. Her eyes were a glowing dark green, and she squinted so hard that Bernie thought she might have been trying to shoot deadly laser beams at him. Sarah continued to press harder and harder and harder onto Mordecai's Adam's apple, while she kept her devilish gaze upon Bernie. She then started to nod her head confidently and coolly up and down, as if she were rocking out to George Thorogood's version of One Bourbon, One Scotch, and One Beer.

The tough leather from the bottom of Sarah's boot finally

released its stranglehold upon Mordecai's neck. Mordecai's feet had kicked their last kick and his fingernails had scraped their last scrape. He lied there on the floor as limp and unresponsive as a drunkard passed out on the sidewalk of the Las Vegas strip on New Year's Eve. Mordecai's lips were stuck in an ashen grey O shape, as if he were trying to blow smoke rings from a cigarette.

Bernie had heard of sleep paralysis, and that was how his body felt now, even though he was more wide-awake than he had ever been in his life. He wanted more than anything to run away from Sarah and her evil boots and to extract himself from that artsy fartsy house, but not a single muscle, tendon, or ligament on his body would budge. Sarah took her first graceful step towards Bernie, then another.

Sarah was less than 10 feet away now, killing the space between them quickly. She had this stupid grin splashed across her face — just the left corner of her mouth turned upward, while the right corner stayed put. Then she was there. Sarah and Bernie were standing nose to nose, with her firm bosom pressing against his dry cleaned shirt with the little polo horsey on the pocket.

Sarah gently placed her forearms over Bernie's neck and trapezius muscles, and he felt the blood flowing to his groin faster than a flash flood during a California mudslide. Her arms were cold, and when she exhaled into his face, Bernie felt no breath. But those eyes. They were so beautifully green that

Bernie felt as if he were becoming Sarah's unquestioning disciple. Sarah's hips started to sway from side to side, and Bernie placed his hands on her lower back, then began rubbing and caressing the top of her ass. Sarah's half smile then became a full smile and she leaned in closely to whisper something into Bernie's right ear. It sounded to Bernie as if Sarah were speaking English, but he couldn't quite tell. The words were mixed and jumbled and Bernie did not know what they meant, but they were the unvarnished sound of black awfulness.

Bernie wept and said NO, NO, NO, but Sarah just kept on talking, as she first moved her left hand, then her right hand, up to Bernie's throat. Sarah kept talking and squeezing Bernie's throat and the things she was telling him were becoming increasingly horrible. Bernie sensed a tingling in his thighs and a weakness in his knees, at which point he collapsed to the wooden floor like a wet rope.

Sarah stood over Bernie with one boot at each side of his ribs. She seemed to quite enjoy the vision of him reduced to a fleshy pile of limp rubble at her feet. With a sigh, Sarah whipped through the doorway and vanished down the hall.

* * *

The next thing Bernie heard was the laughter and chitter-chatter and clinking of glasses at the bottom of the stairs. *THOSE YUPPIE HALF-WITS ARE REALLY GETTING PICKLED.* He picked himself up and brushed the dust from his button-down polo shirt and khaki pants. Bernie's neck was sore and he suspected there were red marks forming a nice little tattoo, so he buttoned the top button of his shirt as if he were a teenager covering a hickey after a summer bonfire at the beach.

A drunken Elizabeth was waiting at the bottom of the stairs to greet her disheveled husband.

"There you are. Where the hell were ya? We all thought that maybe you had flushed yourself down the toilet. Get your ass over here, I want you to meet Terry and his wife Jill, they're both real estate....."

Bernie drifted away from Elizabeth to find Daphne standing at the center of the room holding a great big bottle of something that looked red and warm. Bernie grabbed a clean and empty glass from the dining room table and sauntered over to Daphne, noticing that she actually had some pretty nice curves for a middle-aged gal.

"Fill 'er up, Daphne, and don't be stingy," demanded Bernie.

The red wine went down smooth and hot and Bernie gulped from his wine glass like a man with no class. He stood by himself looking out a picture window at the far end of the dining room as his head became tingly and the blood returned to his face. He sensed that 100 years ago Sarah must've been quite the beauty out there in the vineyard, tending to the grapes in the day and skinny dipping in the pool at midnight under an August super moon.

Bernie guzzled a second full glass of the warm red stuff and enjoyed the calm afternoon, as all the clattering and clinking and small talk at the far end of the house slowly floated away.

Ernie Ballwickle Gets an Idea

ERNIE BALLWICKLE was pleasantly surprised when his hand remained steady as he pointed the gun at the face of the bank teller. He had daydreamed about this for years, and had always imagined that his body would tremble and that the muzzle of the gun would shake uncontrollably when the moment finally arrived. But his body was not trembling and his hand was not shaking and the muzzle of the gun remained focused as if his arm had been chiseled from granite.

It had not been easy finding a bank without plexi-glass protection separating the bank tellers from the customers. Then, one humid and hot afternoon, Ernie Ballwickle drove past Leach Bank on the corner of Mulberry St. and Clarence Ave. Ernie Ballwickle had eased his old brown Dodge sedan into the strip mall parking lot and found a space right next to a handicap spot. He pulled his car all the way up to the wheel stop, put it in park, turned the key back toward his gut, and listened to the old engine gasp and then die.

Ernie Ballwickle tried his best to not look suspicious as he slowly paced up to the bank entrance. He placed his right hand upon a thick wooden handle at the front door, swinging it wide and holding the door open at attention with a smile, as if he were the doorman for the shittiest hotel in California. An older man with a blonde mustache, ostrich skin cowboy boots, and a blue trucker hat reading "Vietnam Vet" walked in past Ernie Ballwickle. "Thank you, kind sir," said the old man. Ernie Ballwickle's .38 special weighed heavily in its holster against his right ankle.

Leach Bank had pathetically been hanging in there since 1980. There had been no remodels or renovations to the interior, which was obvious from the wood-paneled walls and crusty hardwood floors. Nothing separated the customers from the bank tellers but stale, depressing air. An old clear plastic tube labeled "Air Mail" stood as a monument to 1980s inefficiency in the dead center of the room.

The bank teller was a young woman with shoulder length dark hair, large brown eyes, and paper thin lips. Miniature Rubik's cubes swayed and bounced on tiny chains from her taught earlobes. When she first saw the gun, she placed the palms of both hands flat on the desk in front of her, lowered her jaw, and just stared at Ernie Ballwickle as if he were a beautiful sunset.

"Please lady, don't make me use this thing. Just slide the money to me over the counter, then quietly go to the other drawers and collect the rest of the cash. If you do as I say, I'll be out of here in 60 seconds, and you can go about your day. Hell, maybe you and a group of your girlfriends can go down to the beach and have a bonfire tonight and drink beer and make some s'mores. Hey, I like your earrings. Just be careful if you have any young kids at home, because they'll rip those suckers right off," said Ernie Ballwickle with a crooked smile.

She did as she was told, while Ernie Ballwickle slid a backpack off his left shoulder and opened the zipper. Just as Ernie Ballwickle had promised, within about 60 seconds his backpack was full of loot and he was scooting himself out the front door.

"Thank you, ma'am. It's been a pleasure," said Ernie Ballwickle, looking over his shoulder at the young bank teller.

Ernie Ballwickle did not hear any police sirens, but he knew that the fuzz was on its way. They would surely try to get to the bank silently, and sneak up on him. Ernie Ballwickle plopped into the front seat of his Dodge sedan with no license plates and tossed the heavy black backpack onto the passenger seat. He turned on the ignition and slowly made his way south onto Mulberry St.

It didn't take long for Ernie Ballwickle to spot the first police cruiser with sirens blaring, in his rearview mirror. Ernie Ballwickle stepped on the gas and the old Dodge came roaring to life under the hood, reminding him that they don't make cars like the used to. The rumbling of the engine caused the driver seat to vibrate and pushed Ernie Ballwickle's back firmly into the faux leather upholstery.

A second police cruiser joined the chase, which was fine, as long as Ernie Ballwickle could get where he was going with at least a minute to spare before the black and whites caught up with him. Racing straight through the heart of a suburban neighborhood on a Tuesday at 5 PM was not exactly what Ernie Ballwickle had planned. The front doors, garage doors, front lawns, and driveways sped by Ernie Ballwickle faster and faster until he felt like he was on one of those giant circle rides at the fair where they strap you in and spin you around and around until you throw up all your funnel cake onto the poor fellow standing next to you.

Ernie Ballwickle zipped past the last of the houses and hung a sharp left onto Rockfield Blvd. A narrow, winding road paved the way between two aging suburban subdivisions which had been upscale in their day, but were now just clinging to a small amount of remaining dignity. About 200 yards ahead, Ernie Ballwickle spotted his dirt oasis; an overgrown field splitting two sets of track homes with a cluster of tall trees at the center. Ernie Ballwickle stepped on the gas and his old Dodge dutifully shouted a rebel yell that sent blood rushing straight into his loins.

The Dodge thumped over the curb and a new set of Bridgestones tore through the loose dirt and brown weeds of the field. Ernie Ballwickle glanced in his review mirror, and saw the first black and white making a clumsy left turn onto Rockfield Blvd. *These cops drive like a bunch of grannies.* A ragged dirt path along the north end of the field lead the way for Ernie Ballwickle and his Dodge. He was close now. Ernie

Ballwickle stared straight at the cluster of trees and it seemed as if his old Dodge knew just where to go, without the need for him to steer. He rolled down his window to smell the rugged scent of the trees and dirt and weeds, noticing that the yellow banana scented air freshener hanging from his car cigarette lighter had stopped working months ago.

There they were: six holes in the ground. Each tunnel maybe lead somewhere, or maybe lead nowhere. Only Ernie Ballwickle knew the answer. Eight months, that's how long it had taken him. Ernie Ballwickle sat out there every night with his shovel, a bottle of Jack Daniels, a flashlight, and a pack of Marlboros. Drinking, smoking, digging, and pissing. At first Ernie Ballwickle had just planned on digging three tunnels, but eventually decided that six would be safer.

Ernie Ballwickle then had to pick one of the six tunnels for his escape. One of the middle tunnels would have been too obvious. Or would it be? In the end, Ernie Ballwickle finally decided to choose the first tunnel, the one closest to the northern trail that would lead the cars across the field. A blue tarp covered all six tunnels, so no one can see where Ernie Ballwickle would be diving like a hamster running for cover.

The Dodge was still rolling when Ernie Ballwickle stumbled and tripped his way out of the driver's door with his feet kicking and shuffling the soft dirt clods along the side of the trail. The cop cars were gaining on him, but were still about 250 feet away. Ernie Ballwickle had remembered to grab his flashlight off the passenger seat before ejecting himself from the Dodge. The blue tarp covering the six holes was just 20 feet away. Ernie Ballwickle was surprised at how labored his breathing was. His sweating surprised him, too: half moons under his arms, with sweat dripping from his brow and off of his chin. His cottonmouth was so bad that he could barely pry his jaws apart.

The big dirty blue tarp was just where he had left it, draped from the bottom branches of a tree, secured to the ground below. Ernie Ballwickle slithered under the tarp, dove into the first hole, and crawled on his elbows and gut with his trusty flashlight leading the way. In the background, he heard muffled voices at the entrance of the six holes. Ernie Ballwickle had whittled himself down to about 140 lbs., living off of whiskey, cigarettes, and saltine crackers. Even at his size, the escape tunnel was a tight squeeze. *Those cops better be on the Atkins diet if they expect to look for me down here.*

Ernie Ballwickle had forgotten just how long the tunnel was, but he made it all the way through, dragging the backpack full of loot with his left foot from start to finish. He burst through a straw covering at the opposite end of the suburban field. A dirt path would lead him just a few minutes up the road, where a shiny black Pantera was waiting for him on Lake Forest Blvd.

The heat was fading and the sky was transforming into a welcoming shade of orange. Ernie Ballwickle was now officially out of breath, but the backpack felt lighter than ever and he walked with a bounce in the step that only blesses the type of man who has succeeded at an arduous task.

Ernie Ballwickle was never the type of man to press his luck with more bank jobs, but this was just too much fun.

Teresa and the Chaka Ball

THE FIRST THING that truly scared me about Teresa was how hard she gripped the knob on the stick shift of her VW bus. Her grip was not just intense, but appeared desperate and somewhat helpless. That grip of hers would cause the tendons at the back of her hand to rise up against her skin in a way that made me queasy.

And then there was the actual shifting of the gears. Teresa would violently shove the stick shift into place, barely a millisecond after slamming the clutch to the floor with her sandal clad foot. The VW's tired and overworked engine would roar to life, while at the same time beg for mercy, but Teresa just kept pushing and pushing that poor old work horse. The metal stick shift on the VW bus was so long, that I often feared the leverage combined with Teresa's brute force would cause it to rip right out of the floor. Teresa's VW bus would repeatedly take its beatings, while scooting itself on down the road with a surprising amount of remaining dignity. Despite all this, Teresa's intensity was something that had drawn me to her in the first place.

But there was something about Teresa that made me cross. Something intangible, something magical, maybe something a little diabolical. By the time I had sorted all this

---

out, it was too late.

***

It's not often that you meet a girl, and the first thing about her that captures your imagination is her ears. But that's exactly what happened.

I had spotted Teresa at a record store. A real salt of the earth independent record store, probably owned by a couple of guys who spent every night driving Uber until 3 AM to pay the bills. I walked into the shop, happy to get out of the pouring rain, as my Birkenstocks were getting wet and ruined right down to the cork soles.

Walking into a record store always makes me feel uncomfortable these days, because I am no longer young nor hip. Also, I feel uneasy walking into a record store because I know that I will need to purchase at least one record, out of respect for the store owners, and also because I know they desperately need the money from every sale to stay afloat.

The beautiful woman with long, curly, red hair and perfectly shaped gorgeous white ears was perusing through the vinyl collection in the 1980's section. Fluffy red curls were tucked neatly behind each ear, with a few rebel strands flowing like an Irish waterfall over her ear canals. *Great, another beautiful woman with no artistic sense.*

But the truth is, I'm not in any position to criticize another person's musical tastes. No one has ever accused me of being a Renaissance man. My favorite book is Christine by Stephen

King. I just love the way that ugly old red car settles the score for that dorky high school kid with the eyeglasses, by killing off all of his bullies, one by one.

I was headed toward the jazz section, not because I am a poser or because I want to look like a pseudo-intellectual, but because I love all of the jazz piano greats, especially on vinyl. It was probably obvious that I was staring at the girl with the hair and the ears, but I don't remember having the ability to stop myself. The only thing I wanted to know was whether she used Q-tips to get her ears so perfectly clean, or whether her ears were just naturally divine.

I somehow managed to peel my eyes away from the girl just long enough to get over to the record store's halfway decent Oscar Peterson collection. While perusing through Oscar's landmark records, I kept an eye on the girl with my peripheral vision. She had a few albums tucked firmly between her right elbow and her ribs. A thick, smart looking gray sweater covered an even smarter looking white collared shirt. *I'd better think of something clever to say — she looks rather bright.*

I walked in her direction and, if I'm being completely honest, I cut her off in the aisle before she had a chance to make her purchase at the register. As it turns out, I could not think of anything witty or clever to say, so I asked her what she was buying. Without saying a word, the girl with the ears held up a copy of an Ah-Ha album. I made a comment about how much I appreciated their music video, with all of the pencil sketch work and animation that must have been hand drawn. She suddenly smiled and we talked a bit about 80's music, which actually isn't all that bad, now that I think about it.

***

My first date with Teresa was at an Asian food restaurant—one of those authentic joints, where they serve shark fin soup. I'm not an animal rights nut, but that's just wrong. Teresa had a hearty appetite, which I took to be a good sign.

After dinner, Teresa drove me in her VW bus down to San Clemente. All the way to the ocean, I heard something rolling, thumping, and clanking around in the back. She parked right on the sand, with the back hatch of her VW facing the ocean. Teresa twisted the ignition key and let the engine die, then said she wanted to show me something. I said fine, let's see it.

She had me sit at the back of her bus, with my feet dangling over the edge. The night was calm and the moon was bright. Gentle puffs of ocean air caressed my face every so often. The ocean air smelled salty and soft and there was a kind energy flowing from the universe that made me feel like everything would be all right.

I heard Teresa rummaging behind me in the dark, and then I turned around and saw it—a black metal ball covered in some sort of sticky paste. Large metal chains, the kind used for old school bicycle locks, wrapped around it several times. The chains were black, too. There was a smell emanating from the ball that reminded me of the wet, dead trees I had seen many times while hiking in the Pacific Northwest. A musty type of an odor that makes its way into your sinuses and never lets go.

There was a sound, too. A deep and thick hum that made the inside of my skull feel uncomfortable and itchy.

Teresa was sitting on her legs, as if in a yoga position. She stared through the opening at the back of the bus and gazed straight into the ocean. She then looked downward and fawned over the dark ball, with the corners of her mouth turning upward ever so slightly, forming a sinister crescent moon. Her delicate, white, bony hands gently hovered above the ball.

"This is my Chaka Ball," Teresa said, in a trance.

"I have never shared it with anyone, but I want to share it with you. If you touch it, you will see everything you have ever wanted to see," said Teresa.

Teresa was scaring me now, but I was curious. She had this look of horrified ecstasy smeared across her angelic face. Teresa gently lowered her hands, until they were both resting upon the Chaka Ball. Her crystal blue eyes turned a dark shade of green and her thin red curls slowly rose from the top of her head, like a 21st century Medusa.

The sounds coming from her mouth were becoming more bizarre by the second. Then she started speaking in tongues. Maybe she was speaking Latin or Italian, but I'm not learned enough to know the difference. Teresa reached out her hand toward me, and for the longest time I just stared at it. She was wearing a low cut V-neck sweater, and her skin was becoming increasingly luminescent. I had to admit that this was turning me on.

My hands had been folded in my lap, and now they were sweating. I slowly reached my left hand toward Teresa's, slower than molasses, and her green eyes got even greener, her eyebrows pitched upward, and all of her gorgeous red curls shot straight up—some sort of hybrid between a she-leprechaun and Don King.

The moment my finger touched Theresa's hand, I understood. I saw the past and the future blended together into a single black forest of history. There were trees and branches and small spaces of sunlight, with nowhere to go. I saw a vision of myself as an old man, walking with a cane. I also saw myself crying in a crib and wearing a dirty diaper, hearing Chuck Barris babble away like a loony bird on The Gong Show from the TV in the living room of my childhood home. I saw every Christmas, birthday, and Halloween I had ever experienced, all at the same time.

I yanked my finger away from Teresa's hand, then just sat there in the back of her VW bus, catching my breath. Everything was blurry at first, then my vision slowly regained its focus.

Teresa's hands were now smothering the Chaka Ball and

rubbing it as if she were polishing the most rare and precious of pearls. The nonsensical sentences were flowing from her mouth more and more erratically, and Teresa looked as if she were about to break out in tiny little skin volcanoes.

"Come and join us, Stanley. We can always use a fresh set of brains," said Teresa.

I had the most intense urge to springboard from the back of the VW bus and sprint along the cold ocean sand under the night's misty full moon. But what I did was slowly and invisibly move one limb out of the bus at a time, until I was standing with both feet on the sand. I slowly backed away from the bus, keeping my eyes on Teresa at all times. Her eyes locked with mine for a brief moment, and she licked her lips like a thirsty dog.

Teresa returned her loyal attention to the Chaka Ball, and I disappeared, one step at a time, into the black ocean night.

Cabbie In the Orange Grove

THE WORST PART about driving a cab is that people always slam the door when they get out. It was one part of the job that I never got used to.

The date was August 1, 1982, and I still remember it clearly. It was my first day on the job as a cab driver in Orange County. I was fresh out of law school and I had failed the bar examination miserably. When you pass the bar exam in California, you receive a cheerful letter welcoming you to their little club. But when you fail that inhumane three day test, the folks at the state bar make sure to give you a full and complete beating about your test taking deficiencies. According to them, the purpose of such a detailed explanation is to give you pointers to allow you to successfully retake the test. But what I think they are really saying is: *Nice try loser! Don't bother us again.*

Even if I had passed that most medieval of tests, I'm not sure what would have come of my legal career. I didn't go to one of those highfalutin Ivy League law schools like Stanford or Harvard. I went to law school at City College, a law school so pathetic that there were no janitorial services and the students had to take turns at night emptying the trash cans and cleaning the toilets. That should have been my first clue that a successful legal career was not awaiting me on the horizon.

Anyway, there I was, a recent law school graduate turned cab driver with a pregnant wife at home and about seventeen dollars in my pocket. My job was to transport folks back and forth to John Wayne Airport, during the graveyard shift. Business travelers, mostly, along with an occasional woman with tears running down her face heading back to Kentucky or some such place for a funeral for the dearly departed.

My supervisor's name was Woody, and he gave me just a few simple instructions. First, stay out of dark alleys. Second, never leave the cash box unattended in the cab. Seemed simple enough.

My first fare of the evening was a college coed on her way to visit her boyfriend in Alabama. I dropped her off at John Wayne Airport at 8:30 PM, then headed over to Denny's for dinner. I had the Moons Over My Hammy special, which never disappoints. I washed that down with three cups of hot coffee, with three little cups of half-and-half stirred into each coffee. I tipped the waitress four dollars because she smiled at me real nice and called me "honey." Whenever they call me honey or sweetie or anything else that makes me feel tingly inside, they automatically get an extra dollar tip.

I headed back to John Wayne Airport and sat in the queue

until 10 PM. I was reading the latest issue of People magazine (my wife had given it to me). There was a cover photo featuring Burt Reynolds and Loni Anderson. Loni had this great big smile stretching from cheek to cheek, while Burt glared at the camera with just a whiff of hostility or smugness, I couldn't tell which. It was difficult to know what really lied beneath Burt's thick mustache and dark, haunting eyes. My guess was that Loni had invited the folks from People over to the house for an exclusive interview and photo shoot, and that Burt had been dragged along unwillingly.

The vapid articles did not take me long to read, and before I knew it, I was dozing off in the driver seat, with my head fumbling onto my right shoulder.

I was startled out of a deep sleep by the backfiring of an AMC Pacer. Most things in life you get used to, but not the comedic ugliness of that particular automobile. I peered into my rear view mirror and spotted a man walking at a brisk pace toward my cab, carrying nothing but a medium sized duffel bag in his left hand. No luggage. The man had brown, shaggy, curly hair with a brown mustache and mirror aviator glasses covering his eyes. A brown leather jacket covered a pair of narrow, scrawny shoulders. The man was also wearing dark blue Jordache jeans that were so tight that I pondered how any blood could make its way to his crotch.

The man sat down in the backseat of my cab, gently closed the door behind him, and said "just drive." Even as a first day

THEY ARE HERE NOW

cabbie, I knew the dude was bad news.

I merged onto the 405 freeway south, and it was as dark as a pint of Guinness, due to the lack of traffic lights. After about five miles, the man told me where to exit, and directed me through a series of brand new suburban streets where the houses were only half way constructed. After a couple of turns, we were driving through an orange grove and I could feel the tires of my cab slowly rumbling over large dirt clods between endless rows of orange trees.

There was suddenly a blunt pressure at the right side of my neck and I immediately knew that the man was pressing a gun into me.

"Stop here," he said. So I stopped the cab.

"Stay in the cab, and don't go anywhere. If you try to drive off without me you will find out what a good shot I am, so just stay put, all right? Shut off the engine and keep the headlights turned on so I can see what I'm doing."

I found it interesting that he presented his order like it was some type of negotiation, even though he was the one holding the gun.

"Sure, I'll stay right here. Just go do your thing and then let me go," I said. My mouth was so dry that my tongue felt plastered to my teeth.

The man exited the cab with his duffel bag and slammed the door so hard that my inner ears felt as if they had been filled with silly putty. I turned off the engine, but kept the headlights on. The man walked in front of my cab, then fell to his knees about twenty feet in front of the headlights. He slowly and deliberately unzipped his duffel bag, set the gun onto the ground, then started rummaging inside the bag with both hands. He did not take anything out of the duffel bag, which piqued my curiosity more than just a tad. The man retrieved a portable military issue shovel from the duffel bag, and started digging a hole into the soil. He was so leisurely about the digging of the hole that one would suspect he was simply gardening in his backyard on a Sunday afternoon.

The first set of eyes appeared out of the darkness, looking like a couple of fireflies on a mid-west summer night. Then, the gray, furry legs of the first coyote came into view, as my headlights shot straight through the orange groves like a ray gun. The coyotes had been roaming the orange grove in a pack, and in less than ten seconds, there were six of them. The coyotes formed a menacing circle around the man and just stared at him as if they were children enthralled by the tattoo lady at the carnival.

But the man was so focused upon the petty hole he was digging into the earth that he did not notice the coyotes at first. The man eventually looked up to take a breath and wipe the sweat from his brow with his forearm, when he popped up onto his knees with his back as straight as an ironing board.

The coyote closest to the man made a hungry sneer, as a defiant growl was born from its throat. The new housing developments had wiped out the fields and had made the coyotes restless and hungry. Now the coyotes were circling the man and staring at him with their stomachs growling and their frail ribs showing.

The man had dropped his gun and shovel and he was standing halfway hunched over, like someone who had just run a few miles in the heat and was physically exhausted, with his hands on his knees.

Before I had a chance to give much thought to what I was doing, my right hand turned the key in the ignition and my right foot hit the gas at the same millisecond that I put the car in drive. I made a sharp right turn and shot past the pack of coyotes with the man standing at their center. I could see them all in the rear view mirror as the tires from my cab flung dirt clods into the air.

The bright summer full moon painted a not so pretty portrait of the man sprinting between a few of the coyotes before making a run for it. The hungry and desperate coyotes were in hot pursuit of the man, as he frantically hustled for his life with his arms flailing and his jaw hanging so low to the ground that I thought he might trip over it.

It took a few more minutes before I realized that the man was chasing after my cab, hoping that I would stop for him. I considered how absurd it all was, that twenty minutes earlier I was sure he was going to kill me and bury me out there in the orange grove, or at least take my wallet and steal my cab. Now,

I was the man's only hope for salvation.

Oh, what the hell.

I stopped the cab and popped the trunk. The man hopped in, and as soon as I felt the shocks jolt up and down, I hit the gas before the man had a chance to shut the trunk. Dust flew into the coyotes' eyes and the pack parted to the left and to the right, as the man and I sped through the warm darkness.

There was a quaint little bar on the corner of Main Street and Alton Parkway, and the man and I spent the rest of the night drinking Jack Daniels and laughing hysterically. It turns out that the man's name is Casey. He confessed to me the whole story about what was in the duffel bag and why he had me take him to that empty orange grove in the middle of the night, but I am not at liberty to talk about that. I promised Casey that I could keep a secret, and I intend to keep my word.

* * *

Over the years, Casey and I remained fast friends. He was a struggling science-fiction writer and I reviewed the first drafts of a couple of books he was putting together. Most of Casey's stories were not very good, but I told him he was writing some pretty impressive stuff because it must be important for a new writer to develop confidence in himself. But deep down, I think Casey knew that I was putting him on a bit.

We became so close that I was the best man at Casey's wedding. Aside from the family photos of me with my wife and kids, my all-time favorite photo is the one of me and Casey at his wedding, wearing matching black tuxedos with blue ruffle shirts and big obnoxious black bow ties. I sell insurance these days, and that photo still hangs in my office—me and Casey at the wedding with sweaty red faces and bourbons raised high in a toast to good times is quite the conversation starter.

When people come into my office and ask me who the man is standing next to me in the tuxedo, I politely tell them that I don't have enough time to tell the whole story.

THE END

Notes From the Author

I had always wanted to become a writer, but didn't know how to start. One day, at the age of 42, I wrote my first short story. I kept writing new stories as quickly as the ideas came to me. This book is a collection of some of the stories I completed during my first 18 months as a writer. Most of these stories were written late at night, after my three young children were put to bed. I hope my little tales have taken you somewhere.

November 21, 2019

Made in USA - North Chelmsford, MA
1033100_9781708895273
12.07.2019 1602